Island Chain

CHESHIRE PRIZE FOR LITERATURE ANTHOLOGIES

Prize Flights: Stories from the Cheshire Prize for Literature 2003; edited by **Ashley Chantler**

Life Lines: Poems from the Cheshire Prize for Literature 2004; edited by **Ashley Chantler**

Word Weaving: Stories and Poems for Children from the Cheshire Prize for Literature 2005; edited by **Jaki Brien**

Edge Words: Stories from the Cheshire Prize for Literature 2006; edited by **Peter Blair**

Elements: Poems from the Cheshire Prize for Literature 2007; edited by **Peter Blair**

Wordscapes: Stories and Poems for Children from the Cheshire Prize for Literature 2008; edited by **Jaki Brien**

Zoo: Short Stories from the Cheshire Prize for Literature 2009; edited by **Emma L. E. Rees**

Still Life: Poetry from the Cheshire Prize for Literature 2010; edited by **Emma L. E. Rees**

Wordlife: Stories and Poems for Children from the Cheshire Prize for Literature 2011; edited by **Jaki Brien**

Lost and Found: Short Stories from the Cheshire Prize for Literature 2012; edited by **Emma L. E. Rees**

Great Escapes: Poetry from the Cheshire Prize for Literature 2013; edited by **Emma L. E. Rees**

Out of this Word: Stories and Poems for Children from the Cheshire Prize for Literature 2014; edited by **Jaki Brien**

Patches of Light: Short Stories from the Cheshire Prize for Literature 2015; edited by **Ian Seed**

Crossings Over: Poetry from the Cheshire Prize for Literature 2016; edited by **Ian Seed**

Opening Words: Stories and Poems for Children from the Cheshire Prize for Literature 2017; edited by **Simon E. Poole**

Island Chain

Short Stories from the Cheshire Prize for Literature 2018

Edited by
William Stephenson

University of Chester Press

First published 2019
by University of Chester Press
Parkgate Road
Chester CH1 4BJ

Printed and bound in the UK by the
LIS Print Unit
University of Chester
Cover designed by the LIS Graphics Team
University of Chester

A catalogue record of this book is available
from the British Library

ISBN 978-1-908258-34-2

CONTENTS

Contents

CONTRIBUTORS

Melanie Amri gained a BA in Creative Writing with First Class Honours. Her work has appeared in literary magazines, including *Aesthetica* and *Mslexia*. In 2011, she won second prize in the *Mslexia* short story competition. In the same year, she was a winner in The Real Story competition. She has been longlisted for the International Rubery Short Story Award and the Fish Poetry Prize. She is currently working on her short story collection, *Everyone Must Wear Red Shoes on Fridays.*

Elizabeth Brassington was at college in Cheshire, which is still her favourite county. She wrote for girls' comics in the 1970s and has won various short story competitions over the years, including that of *The Sun* newspaper in 2007, with 'Henry'. She has also had poems published in *The Oldie.*

Melanie Cheung grew up and lived in Cheshire until recently. She has a degree in Creative Writing and enjoys writing fiction and poetry in her spare time.

Sophie Claire writes emotional stories set mostly in England and Provence, where she spent her summers as a child. She has a French mother and a Scottish father. She grew up in Manchester and still lives there with her husband and children. After studying Modern Languages at Oxford University, Sophie worked in marketing and proofreading academic papers before becoming a full-time writer. Her hobbies include baking, tennis and sewing. She especially loves making patchwork quilts.

Simon Gotts lived in Chester for many years before moving to the beautiful Vale of Clwyd. His stories have won a number of prizes and have featured in previous Cheshire Prize for Literature anthologies. He has recently published an historical novel, *The Wynding,* about the family of Northumbrian lighthouse heroine Grace Darling. The novel is available from Amazon in Kindle format.

Annest Gwilym is editor of the webzine *Nine Muses Poetry*. Her writing has been published widely, both online and in print. She has won and been placed in writing competitions in recent years. Her pamphlet of poetry, *Surfacing,* is available from Lapwing Poetry. For more information see the *Nine Muses Poetry* webzine.

Angi Holden is a freelance writer and former lecturer in Creative Writing, whose work includes prizewinning adult and children's poetry, short stories and flash fictions. She brings a wide range of personal experience to her writing, along with a passion for lifelong learning. Her family is central to her life, and her research into family history is a significant influence on her work. She was the winner of the inaugural Mother's Milk Books Pamphlet Prize and her poetry pamphlet, *Spools of Thread,* was published by Mother's Milk Books in 2018.

Fiona Holland grew up near Chester and now lives on a smallholding in North Wales. She published her first novel in 2016; *Before All Else,* a year in the life of a Suffolk village and its characterful residents. She is now working on a family saga, *Black Fruit*, due out in 2019. Fiona has won awards for her writing, including the Gladstone's Library Short Fiction prize, and currently teaches Creative Writing.

Chris Hollis-Thompson is a self-published author from Chester. In seven years, he has managed to get four works onto the internet. All remaining works exist in a dusty archive. There's a lock on the archive and he doesn't remember the combination. In addition to writing, Chris enjoys outdoor walking and playing with his son's toys.

Jocelyn Kaye lives in South Cheshire with her husband and children. She has been writing poetry and short stories since childhood and is inspired by art, historic houses and nature. Her fiction has been shortlisted for several writing competitions and her short stories have appeared in national magazines *Prima* and *The Weekly News*. When she's not writing, Jocelyn enjoys walking, yoga and going to the theatre.

Richard Lakin was born in Staffordshire and, after reading chemistry, has worked as a journalist, labourer and police officer on the London Underground. His stories and non-fiction have been published in *The Guardian, The Telegraph, The Oxonian Review* and *Structo* among others.

Sheona Lamont is a pensioner who was born in Easington, County Durham but has lived in Cheshire for forty years. She has written several technical books which remain in print worldwide, but has struggled to write fiction, always becoming bogged down with facts and figures that leave nothing to the imagination. As a result, she does not expect great success but remains hopeful.

Anne Mackey was born in Solihull in the West Midlands. She has been writing poetry and stories for her own enjoyment for many years. She recently took early retirement from a career in libraries and now spends her time writing with a view to publication. In her spare time Anne enjoys playing the saxophone and running (but not at the same time).

Clive McWilliam has lived in Chester for thirty-five years. He was highly commended for the Forward Prize for Best Single Poem and shortlisted for the Manchester Prize, Poetry London and Troubadour International competitions. He has won The Plough Prize, Virginia Warbey Poetry Prize and came third in the 2008 National Poetry Competition. Clive's work has appeared in *The Rialto, PN Review, Poetry London* and *Poetry Review*. His first pamphlet, *Rose Mining,* was published by Templar in 2018. He likes walking, painting and middle distance staring.

John Minshull lives in the beautiful market town of Nantwich, having retired as the Head of Laboratory for Bentley Motors. He has self-published several books on various themes, and one novel, but this is his first 'real' publication. He is a lifelong guitarist and enjoys cycling, table tennis and graphic arts, but his passion is for making and mending; (mostly) managing to re-assemble what he dismantles.

Yvonne Oliver was born and grew up on the Wirral. She began writing a couple of years ago and has been published in Reflex Fiction's *Barely Casting a Shadow*, and in last year's anthology of stories and poems for children from the Cheshire Prize for Literature – *Opening Words.* She loves tennis and reading and hopes to find more time for writing in the future.

Nicola Russell Johnson has a PhD in Creative Writing and has worked for the last four years tutoring postgrads. Two young children mean she doesn't get the chance to have many hobbies and interests right now but her current pastimes include trying to work out what is clogging the sink this time, stepping on Lego® and discovering how long Cheerios can gather under the couch before they become sentient.

Christine Ryan was born in the English county of Monmouthshire, which is now Gwent. She is never sure if she is Welsh or English unless she is watching the Rugby Internationals. She worked for National Museums Liverpool organising educational programmes for all ages. She started writing creatively in 2015 in order to capture her memories of the many adventures she enjoyed worldwide with her husband. She is thrilled to be published in this anthology.

Suzie Sharpe worked tirelessly towards dreams of her short stories being published. By 1998 she was rewarded by being published in many women's magazines including *The Lady*, *Woman's Realm*, *Women's Weekly* and several literary journals. Her career then intruded upon her passion for writing. Twenty years later she has finally returned to what she loves best. She lived in Chester for eighteen years and has now retired to Market Drayton to write full time.

Linden Sweeney was born in Newcastle upon Tyne. She has worked as a teacher and a librarian, latterly at the University of Chester. Linden has attended several writing courses at the University of Liverpool, Gladstone's Library and at The Hurst in Shropshire with the Arvon Foundation. Although her main interest is in poetry, Linden also writes short fiction and, in 2018, she won a prize for flash fiction at the Weaver Words Festival.

Gillian Wallace was born in Sheffield but has sampled many areas of Great Britain because of limitless wanderlust and love of sensational scenery. Discovering and weaving different people and cultures into her writing widens her imagination, she finds. Her poetry has been accepted for anthologies including the 2014 Cheshire Prize for Literature, and she has been published in *Woman's Weekly*. She walks her terrier daily whilst writing stories in her head.

William Stephenson (editor) is Associate Professor of Modern and Contemporary Literature at the University of Chester. He has published numerous research articles and three academic books. His poetry collection *Travellers and Avatars* (Live Canon, 2018) was shortlisted for the Live Canon First Collection Prize. His pamphlets are *Rain Dancers in the Data Cloud* (Templar, 2012) and *Source Code* (Ravenglass, 2013).

FOREWORD

Virginia Woolf once claimed that short stories could be written in either of two ways:

> The great French masters, Mérimée and Maupassant, made their stories as self-conscious and compact as possible. There is never a thread left hanging; indeed, so contracted are they that when the last sentence of the last page flares up, as it so often does, we see by its light the whole circumference and significance of the story revealed. The Chekhov method is, of course, the very opposite of this. Everything is cloudy and vague, loosely trailing rather than tightly furled. The stories move slowly out of sight like clouds in the summer air, leaving a wake of meaning in our minds which gradually fades away. Of the two methods, who shall say which is the better?

The experience of reading over 200 short stories for the Cheshire Prize for Literature 2018 did not help me to answer Woolf's final question – but the many wonderful tales I and my fellow judges were fortunate to read proved her right about the value of the French and Chekhovian methods again and again. Some of the stories were as tightly wound as springs, while others knowingly left their threads of meaning loose.

Whatever approach each writer chose, the best of the submitted stories proved their quality through strong dialogue, description and structure. The spoken words in a short tale should be as few as necessary, so they have room to reverberate, leaving the reader to fill in the silences between the characters' lines. In the strongest of the competition entries, the resonant phrases spoken by the protagonists hinted at hidden inner worlds.

Descriptive passages also need to be brief yet suggestive. In a short story, a sentence outlining what a room looks like, or the smell of an old coat, or the heft of a book in the hand, should be concise and accurate yet must also suggest the invisible emotions, thoughts and sensations that make each character seem human to the reader. In the pieces presented in this anthology, each carefully chosen descriptive phrase acted as a sounding board, creating subtle echoes and intriguing shifts of meaning.

The stories also ended powerfully. Their final lines struck just the right balance between leaving the reader with no further work to do and leaving too much to ponder. Their endings, like those of well-crafted poems, made me want to go back to the beginning and read again.

And this I did. All the pieces in this anthology were studied and discussed many times during the selection process. They represent the very best of the submissions for the Cheshire Prize for Literature 2018. The seven prizewinners and fourteen additional anthology stories were picked from the work of 209 entrants from across the world, all with a present or past connection to Cheshire. The standard was very high indeed; three box files full of deft, daring and thought-provoking stories arrived on my desk in early October 2018. Reading them all in time for the awards ceremony in late November proved challenging but also very exciting. The judging panel was looking for prose that packed a lot into a short space, where characters' lives were tested, striking changes and epiphanies occurred, and language suggested more than lay on the surface.

We were not disappointed. The best of the submitted stories dealt sensitively with difficult topics and made bold narrative moves. We read fictions of domestic abuse, isolation, crime, hallucination and self-discovery, many of which were narrated by outsiders: children, homeless people, victims of dementia, fantasists, even aliens. When read together, the twenty-one pieces in this anthology form an archipelago. Like a ring of islands, they appear separate yet are geologically bonded by strata of language, imagery and theme. Hence the title that sums up their interconnectedness: *Island Chain*.

This year the judges took the unusual step of choosing two winners to receive equal shares of the £2,000 prize, because we agreed that we had two favourite stories of equal merit, both dazzling and deep, yet utterly different. 'Fallen Sparrow' by Sophie Claire showed us a violent, abusive family through the eyes of the young daughter who views her father's alcohol-fuelled aggression and her mother's resistance without fully understanding either. For the baffled, embattled child, the garden swing becomes a portal to the sky; a gateway to danger, metamorphosis and escape. 'Satellites' by Clive McWilliam placed an old man at the edge of a housing estate, watching a dysfunctional family perform a sadistic yet uncannily aspirational experiment on a local dog, in a ghastly mimicry of the 1950s' space race. Both stories touchingly illuminated the plights of their protagonists, and yet achieved far more; they engaged with gender roles, social class, the troubled progress of history and the brutal dynamics of power.

The runners-up prize of £750 was shared equally between five entrants, listed here in alphabetical author by surname: Simon Gotts, 'Tell Us Your Story'; Angi Holden, 'Painting Stones for Virginia'; Fiona Holland, 'Traffic'; Yvonne Oliver, 'On the Dilemma of Whether to Speak Up When Your Baby Vomits into a Stranger's Hood'; and Nicola Russell Johnson, 'Arpeggios of Anxiety'. All these stories showed - with flair, wit and compassion - how the world is seen by protagonists pushed to the margins of the social order: a teenager with separated parents; an old woman living in a nursing home; the driver of a van full of trafficked women; a stressed young mother; and an anxious office worker.

I would like to thank my fellow judges: Peter Blair, an experienced editor, short story writer and publisher; and John Scrivener, a long-standing judge of the Cheshire Prize. A very big thank you also to our fantastic guest speaker at the awards evening, the novelist Zoe Gilbert, who shared with us her ideas on writing, and read the winning stories aloud in a way that brought out all their richness and power. Zoe's experience made her ideally suited to this task: she is the winner of the 2014 Costa Short Story Award and in 2018 published her debut novel, *Folk.* My thanks go also to the High Sheriff of Cheshire, Mrs Alexis Redmond MBE, and her husband, the acclaimed screenwriter Phil Redmond CBE, both of whom spoke eloquently at the awards ceremony to affirm the value of the life of the writer. I could not have completed this anthology without the invaluable aid of Jayne Dodgson, Jenni Davies and Helena Astbury from Corporate Communications, as well as Sarah Griffiths from the University of Chester Press.

Finally, I would like to thank not only every contributor to this anthology but also every author who entered the competition this year. Your hard work and dedication to your craft has created this book.

William Stephenson
Chair, Judging Panel and Editor, *Island Chain*
Department of English, University of Chester,
March 2019

FALLEN SPARROW

Sophie Claire

Bronwen knows her mother will fly the nest one day; she's done it before.

That time she came back, but who's to say she will next time? The slippery blackness of the woods calls to her. The shadows, the sounds, the cold of the night forest won't deter her; anything would be better than here.

She pauses by the back step to examine the twisted shape on the ground. Skin stretched over twig-like bones and a beak too big for its body. Only a dusting of feathers. Looking up at the gap in the eaves, she hears the silence of an empty nest. She saw the parents fluttering in and out, beaks loaded with food; where are they now? The chick stares at the sky through rain-pearl eyes.

Bronwen picks up the rag of flesh and drops it into the bin. She doesn't squirm like the girls in her class would. A farmer's daughter; death isn't what frightens her. Chewing her lip, she lets her feet slap across the path which takes her away from the house.

The mossy air drenches her lungs as she pulls up towards the sky. Toes pointed, she closes her eyes and throws back her head. Fingers wrapped around the rope, she clings on, ready to meet the clouds. The weight of her falls away, her long hair spreads wings behind her and beats a rhythm in her ears. She keeps her eyes fixed on the space between two clouds and aims. Her head, stomach, legs become cobwebs; for a breath-holding moment she hangs in the sky.

This is how it feels to be dead, she decides.

Then her body fills with lead and she sinks back down, her sandals skimming the grass. But Bronwen bends her knees, points her toes, kicks out and swings herself up again. She tugs at the rope as if her life depended on it and pulls herself even higher this time. When she reaches the top, she feels the knife-edge balance; if she tipped any further back she would fall. Her feet draw level with her mother's window. In the bandaged light of her bedroom, her mother might turn her head. Perhaps she will catch the flash of Bronwen's toes or the ends of her hair in the pause before they fall. She will hear the squeak of the rusty frame.

Yesterday, she and her mother made pastry. They rolled two full moons and Bronwen made stars from the trimmings. She watched as her mother slid one circle into the pie dish. Her fingers, quick and gentle, tucked it in and the pastry nestled into the corners. Bronwen tipped in the apples, shook cinnamon. Her mother smiled and winked at her, then she scooped up the other moon and sealed the apples shut.

How does she change so easily from standing tall and solid over the kitchen table, to a pale face shrunk into her bed?

Bronwen's father leaves the barn and rattles the van out through the gates. She jumps down from the swing and runs to the kitchen. The apple pie lingers beside the sink, a wedge gouged out of it. She makes tea and carries the trembling cup upstairs. Her mother is pretending to sleep; pain prevents her from looking at her daughter.

Bronwen rests the cup beside her, whispers 'Mum?' She takes her hand, careful not to touch the redness, 'Will you have some tea, mum?'

Her mother's lids part a little and the colour of her eyes flickers through like the last rays of sunset. When her lips twitch, Bronwen knows this is a smile for her. They sit together, whispering love through their fingertips, trying to silence the noises from the night before.

The pattern she knows by heart: scissored words, chiselled questions, dull thumps. More words, questions, sobbing; like a merry-go-round it spirals, gathering speed until it spins off its axle with a scream and a door slammed shut. But last night was different; Bronwen saw her mother escape.

She heard her mother's feet light on the stairs; the surprise pierced his anger. Through the banister she saw his clenched fists as he went after her. In the time it took him to get his boots on and pick up a torch, her mother had flashed across the field into the woods. Under the cover of black trees, she could have been anywhere. Too late he followed, swinging his torchlight into the branches, but Bronwen knew he wouldn't find her. She watched as he came back, feet weighted with anger.

Much later, Bronwen saw her mother's silky shape slip out from the trees and slide back home. He was waiting, ready to paint her purple with his fists.

'You could have got away,' Bronwen whispers. 'Why did you come back?'

The words squeeze themselves out from between her mother's swollen eyes and split lip: 'For you.'

The sound of the van clattering up the hill makes them both freeze. Her mother shakes her head, waves a hand. *It's not safe,* she always says, *go*. This time she doesn't need to speak, Bronwen understands.

He throws his mud-crusted boots by the door. She makes herself look busy, preparing dinner.

'Your mother not up?' he barks.

Bronwen shakes her head. Her eyes slide up the stairs. The image of her mother's face drops down in front of her like a slide in a projector. She flicks back quickly to the wooden table, and lines up the cutlery like soldiers standing guard over the plates.

They sit in silence. He swallows the ham and bread as if it were the best meal he had ever eaten – better even than her mother's apple pie. The stale beer on his breath snakes across the table and wraps itself around her throat. Bronwen chews the strings of meat until they dry on her tongue, then forces herself to swallow.

'Not hungry?' he asks.

Bronwen shakes her head and nudges the plate away. He pulls it towards him, spears the slice of ham and makes a mouthful of it. The bread bulges in his cheek, then disappears too.

When he puts his feet up in front of the television, Bronwen creeps upstairs with a third plate. She tries to push thumbnail shreds of meat through her mother's lips. But a tear sliding down the side of her nose warns Bronwen to go clear up the dishes.

Then something rouses him from the sofa and he swings into the kitchen.

'Where is she?' he growls, looking through Bronwen. He climbs the stairs and the bedroom door creaks, like a half-healed sore burst open.

Bronwen flings opens the back door and gulps the green air. She throws herself onto the swing, pedals the ground with her feet and runs it up into the sky.

Her mother can't escape this time, the bruises weigh too heavy. But Bronwen knows that when they've healed she will be even lighter than before; her wings grow stronger with every blow he lays on her. She pulls herself up higher. The clouds have knitted themselves together but she pushes towards them anyway, the rope scorching her hands. She needs to find the sky again, the blue world above this cloud-lidded place; she needs to fly.

Waterfalls in her eyes, she lets go. And when she tips back, she doesn't see the clouds falling away, the earth coming up to catch her. Her bones fold flat against the ground; a small pile of twigs beneath an empty swing.

SATELLITES

Clive McWilliam

The first creatures in space were fruit flies who made it back to earth by parachute just after the war. Two Russian tortoises circled the moon and dogs were grabbed from the streets in the 1950s. Bitches were best, it is said, as they wouldn't have to cock their legs in space.

Mark Mapp folds the wet newspaper and squints through the broken window towards the estate. There is a half-brick on the table where he sits. A light over the marsh behind him flickers in the corner of his one good eye like a scratch on a lens. Mark Mapp didn't sleep well last night. All this talk on the wireless about Sputniks. 1960. It's another world. Woke up with a pulsing blue light which seemed to have blown in on the night's high wind. A police car outside the Yaps' house and a stray dog barking. Some nonsense with a firework.

He's so thin, the evening light shines through him as he looks across at the tower of tyres in the Yap family garden. The last tower had burned for two days last backend. During their first winter here on the estate the Yaps had run out of firewood. Now their new house has no internal doors and the skirtings are almost gone. Mark Mapp brushes ginger biscuit crumbs from the front of his smock. Lights up a Woodbine and looks down at the marsh.

His two-room hut is a patchwork of breeze block and wood, wind whistling through. A smear of cement and green paint across its tilted sides. Corrugated roof that chimes in the rain. Underpinned with larch poles driven into the peat two hundred years before, that show themselves like wader birds' legs during dry weather. There are two wicker chairs, a camp bed and pine table his grandfather made. On a wall a photograph of a couple sitting with a blurred baby on a beach. The room smells like the inside of old hats. A room below is stacked with seed potatoes and cartridges. There's a tin shower cubicle full of spades and daffodil bulbs. All the fields to the east have been stuffed with council houses. Built since the war for young families corralled from the town, leaving their Victorian terraces to demolish themselves.

Mark Mapp still keeps a gun in the gutter below his house. His gun is a curiosity. The barrel a bell-mouthed Chinese jingal he'd bought in Shanghai. The lock from a Sevastopol musket and the whole is bound together by wire to a homemade stock. He'd once had this fowling area to himself. Life had revolved around morning, evening and tide flights. Cheviot sheep thrived on the saltings and extended the short sward favoured by geese and widgeon. His fenland punt was open decked and could not go out to sea. Years ago he'd begun a boat, to take him further out. It is still rooted against the gable of his hut. Weather has curled its plywood bows. The deck is a bed of reeds which drum in the wind.

He rarely saw anyone then. Small boys might have waved as they passed on their bikes with fishing rods. There might be a shot from another fowler's gun. But after the war, the air coarsened. A knock on his door would not be for a glass of water. There have been times when he's fired his Chinese jingal over the hedge at the estate.

Last night's stray dog is still barking outside. A rind of a thing with a harness around its shoulders, barking at the Yaps in the road. 'Bloody Sputnik dog!' they shout. The dog holds its ground as they throw stones, then it runs down the track to Mark Mapp's hut to drink at the puddle outside his door.

Mark Mapp leans into the window as a flight of oystercatchers darkens the sky. The whiskers around his mouth move, silvery, as if he is trying to make sense of the distance; sunlight playing on gullies of salty water, trying to speak to him.

His first memory is of the R101 looming over the marsh during the Great War, lost. He had run to tell his mother but it was gone by the time he found her. Never trusted his own perceptions since. His sisters had started calling him Blimp.

Outside in the road someone is singing *Cathy's Clown*. Spinner Yap has one of his brothers in a headlock. Spinner's limbs are unusually long and his head unusually small. Sunlight shines through his ears. The stray dog is barking and squats behind a bin as they throw stones. Spinner is wearing industrial rubber gloves and another Yap has a shopping bag.

Mark Mapp wonders if this must be Thursday, when Syd comes. His grocery van distorting the houses in its shiny sides like a hall of mirrors. Syd, circling the town with provisions for outlying farms and the new estates, bringing him ten Woodbines, biscuits, a twist of tea. Thursday, when Mark Mapp can open the door again for a while.

'What are those birds there?' Syd will ask and he will tell him that some are Redshanks, the others are Seapies and those others whistling are Widgeon.

Spinner Yap is pushing the stray dog into a cardboard box. The animal is a blur of rage. Another brother has grabbed the dog's back legs while a third has pulled the shopping bag over its head to stop it biting. Through his field glasses, Mark Mapp watches the Yaps walk out to the pylon on the marsh. They carry the dog in the box and a bed sheet by its corners which flutters like a flying carpet. Mark Mapp leans on the sill, holding his breath as if taking a shot; as if not to disturb what they're doing. Their distant braying. The rush of marsh grass and incoming tide.

They climb the pylon halfway and wrestle with the sheet as they tie it to the dog. Sheep regroup below. The dog's familiar bark is carried on the wind as they pull the shopping bag from its head and lob the whole bundle from the pylon. Their cheers are like a burst of geese rising laden from the fields. Their bed sheet parachute billows and spins and holds the dog over the marsh for a countdown of five, then plummets behind a hedge.

Mark Mapp picks up the newspaper again from the table. Shakes it straight. The oily carpet sparkles with grains of glass like estuary sand.

Early next year, the United States will launch Ham the Chimp into space in a Mercury capsule. Ham has been trained to pull levers to receive rewards and avoid electric shocks.

TELL US YOUR STORY

Simon Gotts

So I was like will medad be able to hear this cos he thinks im lyin about being on the radio. An the presenter said where does he live an i said chorley why. An then hes like he wont hear it there we only go out to cheshire and a bit of wales but he can download it as a podcast an im like no he cant cos he dont know one end of a smart phone from the other. I thought i was going to be nervous but the studio was nothing just like a little room with brown glass windows an you could still see the trucks going past on the dual carriageway.

I wanted medad to listen cos he used to love x files an that but i dont live with him now i live with mum an her boyfriend fee short for feenix but its not his real name. Mostly ive no money on my phone so i use the one by fees computer when they go to mindfulness. Sometimes medad cries then i cry too an no way im letting them hear.

So the presenter says just tell me in your own words what happened to you yesterday morning. You were walking your mothers dog by the canal. So i told him about how one minute i just let kyron off his lead an he was doing his business an the next moment i was lying on like this surfboard an kyron wasnt with me no more. And then what happened the presenter says. His name was garry i think or it could of been barry i never heard right cos my hearing aids were making that whistle an i had to turn them down cos he said the engineer would have his guts for garters. I said thats when i saw them they had egg shape heads an big green eyes an long arms with black fingernails like claws an hes like who an im like the aliens of course it wernt ant an dec.

He was nice the presenter. He had blue eyes not big green ones an a check shirt an fancy boots like woody off of toy story. So hes like what did they do to you an then he waves to the engineer to stop recording an says if it was anything intimate by which i mean dirty we better just skate over it as this show goes out at drivetime and there could be families listening. I said my family wont be listening an hes like no but others might be so i said no they never did nothin like that anyway. I dont know why he asked except maybe he wanted to know himself. Medad says pedos is everywhere.

So then this lady i talked to when i first got to the studio an i thought was a volunteer like they have where I do my gardening comes in with cups of tea an penguins an the presenter says would you rather have hot chocolate an im like no thankyou i always have tea three sugars. People think they have to decide for me but i know what i like ive a mind of my own is what medad says. Fee says the same but its different when he says it. Medad cant have me because he didnt have a job when the judge decided an he drank special brew an watched jermey kyle. I used to sit on the sofa next to him an cuddle up close for in the night garden an hed microwave donuts to keep us warm. Id be like will mum be cross when she gets home an hed be just oh never mind her shes a effing bee.

The presenter asked me what the aliens was wearing. I said just skin. They had silver skin very smooth no wrinkles or hair. Shrink wrapped like in the supermarket he said. Yes i said only it wernt plastic it was their skin. And did they let you get off the surfboard he says. I said yes they took me to a little room all grey with eggboxes on the wall an they made me talk into this machine with a bit on the end like a frying pan. So hes like could you understand what they said an im like i understood what they told me to do but when they talked with themselves it was like romanian or something. Were there just the two of them he says yes i said a man alien an a lady alien. And were they kind to you he said well i said i dont know if they was or not they just told me what to do all the time an they had no lips to smile with. They kept me for two weeks an we flew over blackpool tower one time an i said to them i wish i could still go there with medad but they never said nothing. So he says did they give you any food or drink all this time. An i dont really know but im trying to answer the question so i say yes they gave me a pink drink in a paper cup an it made me sleepy. And you woke up back on the canal towpath he says and it was only the day after you were taken. Do you think it was a spaceship you were in. So i say yes what else could it of been because they had to come all the way from another galaxy didnt they. An he laughs really loud like id made a joke. Sorry he says an holds up his hand. An im like no worries but the engineer gives him the finger from inside his glass box.

He takes me back to the green room which isnt green just grey an brown like everywhere else. He says tracey will get you a hot chocolate an then hes like it was lovely to talk to you fantastic listen out on friday about four thirty thats when itll be on if selected. So the volunteer lady comes in with my drink that i didnt ask for an i can hear him whispering to her but dont know what he said. She sits down next to me on the squeaky plastic. Close up shes dead old like fifty. She has grey streaks an her skin comes off like snowflakes when she rubs her hands. She says look i repaired your glasses i didnt know kids listened to the radio these days i thought it was all youtube and whats up i dont know why the green room has to be the coldest room in the building do you have a lift home i gave your dog a biscuit but he was sick. An im like no i walked here. Ten miles on your own she says an im like yes on my own im sixteen an its whatsapp. Sixteen she says well i suppose thats all right then if your old enough to have sex. I said i dont have sex an shes like sorry sorry didnt mean it like that but why have you said all this about being abducted by aliens do you think its true. An im like no its not true well most of it int true the bit about takin kyron for a walk was true i just said it cos my social worker has the radio on in her car an when she hears it theyll send me back to medad.

So shes like why would they do that an im like because it shows mum an fee dont look after me properly if an effing great alien spaceship comes down an takes me away an they never do nothing about it. So then she takes hold of my hand. I dont want you to be disappointed she says but it may not go out on the air because the tell us your story spot is supposed to be for real life experiences. An then im like i could tell you a true story an she says im already in the dog house for letting you over the threshold in the first place. But ive had loads of real life experiences i said. An then shes like yes but not ones people want to hear about when theyre making an early getaway for the weekend. So she takes me an kyron home.

Now im in shit for staying out all night cos fees been all round the neighbours askin if they seen me an kyron. He took the goodie bag off me cos it had plastic an refine sugar but i hid the badge in my secret treasure place so he never found that. If i twist myself round i can read it from my bed. It says I TOLD MY STORY ☺

PAINTING STONES FOR VIRGINIA

Angi Holden

'There you are, Esme,' the woman says, with a tinkling laugh. 'We thought we'd lost you!' She places a cup of tea on the round table beside my chair. There is a girl with her.

'Hello, Gran,' the girl says. She bends forward and places a soft kiss on my cheek. Her lips are warm and her eyes twinkle. She reminds me of my Albert, but I don't see him very often these days. I'm not sure where he's gone.

'Would you like a cup too?' the woman asks. The girl thanks her and smiles. She has been brought up well. I like her.

'What have you been doing today?' she asks, as she takes off her coat and drapes it across the back of a chair. She sits down and takes my hand in hers. It feels comfortable. There's not much touching in my life now. I miss Albert's cuddles. There isn't even a cat to stroke.

'I've been chatting to Virginia,' I say. 'She's not very well. She gets depressed.'

'I don't think I know Virginia,' she says. 'Is she the new lady with the curly hair?' I try to think who she means, but I haven't seen anyone like that. Maybe I'll meet her another day. Not many people come out to the conservatory now the summer is nearly over. They say it's a bit chilly, but it isn't. There are radiators and everything. It's a very good hotel.

'No,' I say. 'Not new. I've known her most of my life. A plain woman, with her hair scraped back in a bun.' I lean forward so that nobody else can hear me and whisper. 'She's got a bit of a big nose.'

The girl chuckles.

The woman comes back with a cup of tea for Jenny. Yes, that's it. Jenny.

'Has Esme been telling you about our painting?' she asks, as she places the tea next to mine. It's got less milk. I think I might prefer it. The girl shakes her head. I think she's read my mind, but then I realise she's answering the woman.

'We've been painting stones. It's all the rage, you know. The residents paint them and then some of the staff put them around the town for people to find.' The woman smiles. 'There's a website and everything,' she adds.

Jenny says she's seen something similar where she lives. People record where they've found these stones, and then hide them somewhere else for other people to find.

'Is it a game?' I ask. And she says it is. Sort of.

I pick up the cup and take a sip. It's hot. Not like that milky one. That's beginning to skin over. Too much milk.

'Did I tell you Leonard came to see me today?' I ask the girl. She shakes her head. 'A nice man. A bit dour and humourless, but very kind. He has a lot to contend with, of course. With that wife of his.'

'I don't think I know Leonard,' the girl says. 'Does he live here?'

'We haven't got a Leonard here,' the woman says. She looks puzzled. 'I don't think your Gran has had any other visitors today. Although it might have been earlier in the week, of course.'

'No, it was definitely this morning.' I don't like being contradicted. 'He sat here in the conservatory and read to me. It was a new book, he was very proud of it. He's a publisher, you know.' The woman shakes her head and smiles a secret sort of smile. I don't like it when they do that. It's like they know something I don't. I'm glad when she goes.

'What was the book, Gran?' says the girl. I can't remember her name. I can't remember the book's name either, but I can see it on the windowsill. The girl picks it up. It's well worn, so it can't be the one after all. '*To the Lighthouse*,' she says. 'I read it at uni. I loved it.'

She must be quite bright. I taught students once, and you could tell the bright ones. They were always reading. She puts it down again, next to some painted stones. I wonder if I've told her we painted stones today. There was a woman with a lot of stones from the beach, and pots of paint. They encourage us to attend the art classes in the hotel lounge. I quite enjoy it when I'm in the mood.

'I bet you painted this one.' The girl picks up a stone with a bright yellow and black bee on it. I don't understand how she could know, but she's right. I love bees. Albert used to keep hives at the bottom of the garden. I wonder where he is now. Maybe he's down there now, in his white suit with his puffer. It doesn't do to get stung.

I finish my tea. She hasn't drunk hers. I'm not surprised. It did look too milky. She comes and sits beside me.

'I won't be able to come and visit for a while,' she says. Her eyes are a bit glittery. 'I've met someone. His name is Jonathan. We're going off travelling for a month or so.' Her features have changed, softened. 'I'll come and see you as soon as I get back.'

'I'll be fine,' I tell her. She seems to need reassuring. 'Vita will come and see me. She's a one for travelling, always talking about Paris and Rome and places.'

The girl gathers up my cardigan and starts to tuck it around my shoulders. There is a heavy clunk.

'What's this?' she asks. She digs in the pocket and takes out three big stones. 'Oh Gran, you don't want stones in your pockets.' She takes them out and puts them on the windowsill. She kisses me and then waves from the door as she leaves.

She's right, I think. Stones are not a good thing to keep in your pockets.

There's always a risk of drowning.

TRAFFIC

Fiona Holland

Once on the road, he remembers the young lad in the van hire place.

'Everyone's suspicious of white vans these days. Since that fella drove into the crowd outside the mosque. Know what I mean?'

The lad talked to himself as he selected buttons on the photocopier. 'Press here to Copy.' He pressed with an exaggerated flourish. 'Yay!' The machine whirred into life and a blue light tracked beneath the driving licence and insurance documents. Nine points, six due to expire next month. 'There you go, sir. Moving house, is it?' He didn't answer, tucking the documents the lad had slid back over the counter into his inside pocket. 'I'll just go over the vehicle with you before letting you get on your way.'

Traffic is slow. Vans from everywhere. Wallasey. Wigan. Chester and Wrexham. Bootle. It's dark and people are leaving work. Worker ants scuttling home. Cocks of the walk burning the midnight. Stop start stop start all along the A57. At the traffic lights, smells from the takeaways drift in through the open air vents. Polish. Persian. Bangladeshi. Chinese. He could really do with a kebab, but he's got a timetable to stick to.

First pick-up's already in the sat nav. Drop-offs and other pick-ups to be notified. No van driving more than a hundred miles. Keeping it local. As the lad said, you're never going anywhere 'nice' in a white van. It's strictly business. If you're not moving your gear or moving gear for some mate, you've had to hire a van because your own wheels are off the road. MOT advisory. Some div in a 4x4 ran into you and you've got to get the chassis fixed. Insurance write-off, waiting for the cash. Any number of reasons. Ask the boss, mate. Just doing my job. His other car's a Porsche.

He's finally out of the city. It's dark, but he knows the layout of the land. Rolling hills. Turbines. Slow canals. Occasional distribution hubs dropped on the landscape like extra-planetary cities. He's done this route loads of times. Just doing his job.

Usually it's industrial estates. Sometimes backstreet pubs, farm buildings, canalside warehouses, nightclubs, caravan parks. If it's a new place, the trouble is finding it. Postcodes in the countryside can go on for miles. Usually there's some bloke with a torch flagging you down. He knows what van you're driving because somebody's already messaged ahead with the registration plate.

Makes him a bit uncomfortable, that. That feeling of being watched. It's a tight operation, one of those where you just know your bit. If you found out too much, well, you could get shot. Could get shot anyway, he supposes.

The thought makes him shift uncomfortably in his seat. He'd been thinking about stopping at a garage. Comfort stop – pick up a sausage roll and a can – but now the thought of the warm pink rendered meat is making his stomach lurch.

There's a big moon, low to the horizon. Its brightness makes it a hub in a wheel of light. Fast moving, scruffy clouds polish its face.

First stop turns out to be an old camp, one of those that used to house prisoners of war. He parks by a gap in the fence between two decayed concrete posts. Shoots of larch or birch whip in the wind, catching the corner of his eye like scurrying figures. No one comes, so he slides out of his seat and walks round to the back of the van. The door creaks as he pushes against the wind. It holds fast on its double-jointed hinges. It's cold, so he gets back into the cab, wedging the driver door open with his foot to keep the light on.

The van shifts as he feels the load weighing down the back. A girl climbs in beside him as a man appears at his window, hood pulled up, deep shadows only defining his face.

'How many, mate?'

The man nods to his new companion and says, 'Four, plus her,' and gives him another postcode which he taps in. The girl nods her head, her lips moving as she repeats it for him. The doors slam and the van booms to the man's pounding knock as they drive away.

They travel in silence. She's occupied by her phone. He hears answering beeps in the back of the van.

She coughs. He looks at her, looks first at her thin leg outstretched to the dash board, ending in a pink flip flop. Her toes are tiny and deformed, must be cold too, in this weather. She answers his look appraisingly.

'The girls are hungry. We want to eat.'

'Hey. I've got a schedule to keep. Can't stop.'

'Please. Hungry.' He catches a glimpse of her furrowed forehead as she bends to a bag on the floor. 'We've got money.'

'All right. At the next service station.' She nods and texts. Her phone beeps back almost immediately. She shows him a picture on her screen. It is dark and grainy, not much detail. He can just make out a few heads together, hair mingling, big smiles and raised thumbs.

'Here's the deal. I'll get it. You lot stay in the van. And bloody keep quiet.'

'Sure.'

He pulls off the motorway and parks between the shops and the petrol station, a dimly-lit area of pick-up trucks and massive garbage bins. He puts one finger to his lips and makes a shushing sound, hoping she will relay to the others the need to be absolutely quiet. She obviously doesn't get it because she bangs loudly on the wooden partition and speaks rapidly and liltingly. There's a correspondingly loud bang from the back. God, why does he bother?

He hurries across the oil-bright tarmac pulling his coat around him against the chill wind. He then hurries back again with six pasties, six bottles of water and six KitKats. Extracting two of everything, he throws the flimsy carrier bag into the back through a narrow gap in the doors, flapping his hand into the dark space to indicate they should make no noise. Someone in the dark void of the van grabs his hand. He pulls it away sharply, catching the inside of his wrist on the door catch. He sucks the blood.

She eats like a rodent, taking small bites and chewing with her front teeth. She holds her cheek as if her teeth hurt. Probably rotten.

There are squeals of protest as he takes off again at speed and hurtles down the slip road, joining the forward rush of traffic. She nods and pulls her coat around her and leans her head against the window.

She's bony. Her knees are bony. Her feet ridged like a ploughed field. Thin straps. Too much gap between strap and flesh. Her phone, which is lying between her fingers and her thigh, buzzes mutely. A picture of two young children lights up. Her fingers twitch and then lie still. She must be fast asleep.

Twenty? Twenty-two? At a guess, he'd say Eastern European, possibly Croatian. The tight parallels of her intense, dark eyes. Hollowed cheeks. Straight, straight hair. Lines grooved into her thin face as if pressed there by thumbnail. Everyone knows they are from almost any other place than here. But what will be journey's end for these girls? What happens when the stunts get harder and harder? What happens when they start to look like our home-grown sisters on the street - waxy skin, toothless mouths, wild eyes, unprotected for that £20 heroin fix?

But, hey, that's not his problem. Why is he even thinking about it? Eyes on the road.

He drives round to the back of a packing and distribution warehouse. Roller shutters lift just enough to allow a man to crouch and peer out. The shutters open fully and a white van drives out. The man mimes for him to turn his engine off. He is short and stocky and walks with his elbows turned inwards as if his upper back is packed with fat.

Two men and a woman appear, handing out the girls who stand in a huddle. The girls move and mingle, touching one another, laughing into the cold air, brushing flakes of pastry from their clothing, strands of their hair blowing into each other's mouths. His travel companion slides out of the cab to the ground. Before she closes the door she turns back to look pointedly at him, and shrugs. 'Hey, doll,' he wants to shout. 'What d'ya mean?' She waggles her phone at him and points to the sat nav, mouthing the postcode over and over.

An intense white light burns like magnesium. Rough hands pull him from his cab. His feet skitter over gravel. Someone is talking in a monotone, but he can't hear the words. Now *he* is sitting on the floor in the back of a van, his fingers threaded through metal mesh.

Just who had she called?

ON THE DILEMMA OF WHETHER TO SPEAK UP WHEN YOUR BABY VOMITS INTO A STRANGER'S HOOD

Yvonne Oliver

It's a quandary. Her first instinct is to bail at the next stop, but she's only just recovered from the challenge of collapsing the buggy in the first place, queueing passengers tutting her into error, and does not feel up to the challenge of unfolding it. Her hip has yet to discover quite the correct jut for baby perching, and that casual one-handed wrist-flick every other mother seems to have mastered, which sees the broken bat buggy transform into the perfectly designed transport of choice for squalling pink bundles of sleep deprivation, is still beyond her.

On the opposite side of the bus is a model mum – her baby sits contentedly on her lap and doesn't squiggle or grab at her long smooth hair, and they have matching rosebud complexions, the type she imagines you get by eating organic and getting twelve hours' sleep a night.

She wonders why such mothers frequent the bus, as surely, they all drive cute but trendy little Minis or VWs. Perhaps, on government request, they take monthly bus trips to subtly demonstrate to the lower order mothers how they should be doing things. Or maybe like her they have failed their driving test twice already and have come to realise that polluting the planet is a selfish act, the worst sort of example to set these miniature homo-sapiens emissions who emerged into this world to your screams and their own. Unless of course you are a

Scientologist mother, who apparently elects to do it in silence, according to the article in *All Talk* magazine. Once it would have been a work of literary fiction, a Pulitzer-winning something or other, well okay, a novel at least, but completing a paragraph amidst high decibel infant demands is now a victory, so short sensationalist magazine articles are more her bag.

She ponders how those Scientologists had a choice at all, considering the bellows expelled from some primordial cave deep in her subconscious, totally undermining her six-page efficiently typed Times Roman font double-spaced birth plan, which specified a natural water birth, with no pain relief other than controlled breathing. She'd been an absolute star in prenatal classes, the first thing she'd ever shone at, even beating the lesbian lady with the super-stylish cropped haircut who was at a MASSIVE advantage as her birth partner was a woman, not a clueless bloke who kept checking the football score on his mobile.

In all fairness, on the day, Josh had actually maintained his panting control far better than she had, and it was quite unfortunate that he'd keeled over in a dead faint, submerged in the paddling pool. Not quite what she'd envisioned when she'd opted for a water birth, but realistically how DID she think they were going to accommodate a palm-fringed infinity pool in the centre of the John Radcliffe? It was a pity that the video footage was all destroyed, but in truth it was going to need some pretty heavy expletives editing, and she was secretly relieved all evidence of her humidity-challenged hair had been eradicated.

Dilemma contracts her pelvic floor, reminding her of those neglected exercises – one person in the family with bladder control issues is quite enough – thoughts flit to potty training: where do you even start? She is beginning to feel nauseous herself. She imagines tapping Hoody boy on the shoulder, him turning, pulling out an earbud …

'Excuse me, I'm so terribly sorry, but my baby has been bilious in the hood of your jacket,' sounds like something from an Agatha Christie BBC production. She pictures herself in a 1920s' cloche hat – useful for disguising her unbrushed hair, but hideously ugly too. She does not have to say anything but is aware that the soft hiccup and subsequent aqueous splat may have alerted other passengers to the situation.

She's pretty sure the bent old gent with the trilby and one pink sock, one tartan is an ally – mismatched socks are a clear sign of a disordered life her mother has always said, so he's sure to identify. She herself is wearing no socks at all as going up the stairs one more time after the foray for baby wipes, then a buggy-sized blanket, then sunscreen – just in case – and the last-minute dash back up for a bra, left socks in the same compartment as stockings and suspenders – frivolous fripperies, a fond memory but of very little use in this new world of nappies and teething and vomit. Although her sock HAD come in useful as an extra breast pad at the mother and baby group – turns out her frantically lactating breasts were as incapable of discerning her own baby's cries as she had been at the hospital – the unfortunate incident of the mistaken baby – it was wearing the exact same Babygro and Alfonso from the covered market had sworn, SWORN it was a unique item or she would never have paid thirty quid (twenty if Josh asked) in the first place: it was an honest mistake!

Perfect mum is trying to make eye contact – she must have seen. It was a mistake to get on the bus in the first place – why hadn't she just walked? Exercising the dog was in her top ten *Things to Do* on the magnetised jotter Josh had helpfully purchased – with its pen on a string so she wouldn't lose it – he'd proudly pointed out. He hadn't been so pleased with himself when he'd come home to find numbers 16 to 23 permanently daubed on the fridge itself – who knew! A fridge door and a white board are easily mistaken by day thirty-four of a slumber-less stasis – particularly as number 22 was 'Haemorrhoid cream', with three asterisks and a sad face.

It's his fault anyway. Sarah had obviously inherited his genes – Saturday mornings were for lie-ins as far as she was concerned, but Josh was always up with the birds for his 10k jog. It was small comfort that at least he too was slowed down by the arrival of Sarah – it took him way longer these days. Unless of course ... Oh God, he's having an affair! And who could blame him – his wife is a nipple-dribbling, crazy-haired zombie who is never intending to have sex again, EVER.

Stay calm, remember he's also developed a keen interest in gardening, he's probably just avoiding being home with her and Sarah – the bastard! Is it worse if he leaves her for another woman or because even being alone is better than this? And what about Sarah – she'd be a single parent … but what if Josh went for custody … she couldn't live without Sarah … but she'd have sleep … she is a bad, bad person.

It is too hot on the bus and Sarah is wriggling to stand again, her tiny feet slipping on her probably soon-to-be-abandoned mother's wobbly, thigh-gapless legs. Her still-convex belly is wobbling with the vibrations of the bus – model mum's baby MUST have been preemie, it's only the same size as Sarah, yet her stomach is as flat as her GHD'd hair. It's so unfair – she had been exercising for MONTHS yet people were still asking her when it was due. Well maybe not months, but weeks at least, when she had the time … and the energy … she definitely, distinctly recalled at least six very athletic star jumps and under the circumstances that's pretty impressive if she says so herself. Josh is lucky to have her.

The brakes squeal and there is a welcome puff of cold air as the doors slide open. Hoody boy stands, squeezing into the aisle as the bus gives a final shuddering exhalation, and everyone lurches. Sweet odd-socked old man stumbles into Hoody boy who shoves him back and tells him to F-off! Odd socks flushes, automatically apologising, but Hoody boy doesn't hear him, or all the tuts: he's still ear-plugged. He steps lightly from the bus.

As the bus pulls away the first drops of rain hit the window, veering sideways as the bus gains speed. All eyes follow Hoody boy as he continues jauntily along the pavement, reaching back for his hood. Perfect mum grins at her, revealing a grotesque snaggletooth, and there is a communal sense of well-being as she sits in the warm humming body of the bus hugging Sarah close.

ARPEGGIOS OF ANXIETY

Nicola Russell Johnson

It was a relief when I got the job. Last month's rent was paid by selling my microwave and accepting £30 for writing questionable fanfiction about women wrestlers for a guy online with a tights fetish. I love my flat too. It's just one room but it's mine, it's clean and if you don't overdo it on the paper when you wipe, the toilet flushes almost every time.

Today's day one. I'm wearing polyester; or as I call it, Satan's satin. It's making me sweat so hard I've had to stick panty-liners to my armpits. The job is a support helpline for a small payroll software company. Honestly I've no idea what any of that means, but they hired me, so they're great.

The company's situated in a business park that looks half 1970s' council estate and half post-apocalyptic wasteland. A breeze blows empty Wotsits packets over my £5 shoes that don't fit and slip off every step. I tried sticking Blu Tack to the inside heel, but it hasn't worked and has melted and now I look like I've got a fungal problem.

Karen, the manager, is pleased to see me though. She shakes my hand so enthusiastically a panty-liner comes unstuck. I'm handed a pamphlet, told to read it, try out the software and then when I'm good and ready, to start answering calls.

Like it's that easy.

Then she hands me over to a guy called Jim.

Jim's in office casual and a beanie and he seems like a good guy. He introduces me to the other people in the office. Janet's on the phone working. She's wearing cheap black trousers with yoghurt stains and has a grubby looking dog.

I'm told that Janet got divorced last year and she's really mean to the customers. She once told a guy to post her his Cheerios so she could be the second person to piss in them that day. She didn't get suspended but now she's got a support dog. I'm told he'll grow on me but not to pet his back legs because he's got a weird rash.

The other person is Chris. Apparently he takes a shit at 10.30 every morning for forty-five minutes but it's best to stay away for at least an hour. He's got two kids, three jobs and can get you frozen food cheap if you ask him.

I wave and try not to think about his bowels.

Jim says the toilets are gender-free and not to use the third one, because like that Japanese horror story, a guy died in there. His name was Shane and a couple of months ago he overdosed on cocaine on a Friday and nobody found him until the next Monday when Chris went in to shit. Only Jim tells me he went in first thing Monday and swears Shane had shouted 'YES?' when he knocked on the door. So now nobody uses that cubicle.

Great.

He shows me my desk, signs me into the computer and apologises for the noise from the builders.

I can't hear anything. It's just me, Chris, his brewing bowel movement, Janet and the dog. The office is silent apart from mouse clickings and mumbled conversations.

Then I'm left at my desk with the pamphlet. It's the manual the customers get when they buy the software.

So pretty much they're going to be phoning someone who impressively knows even less than they do.

Great.

No wonder Janet has to bring a support dog and threaten to piss in people's Cheerios, and Chris has to empty his bowels for forty-five minutes every day, and Shane, poor dead son of a bitch, had to snort crack in the toilet and answer from the other side every time someone needs to take a shit.

I think of my beautiful little flat. The sink quit working last week but it's okay because it turns out it's fun to wash the dishes in the shower.

So, payroll software.

What do I know about payroll software?

I know nothing about payroll software.

I spend the day fannying about on the computer, putting numbers in little boxes and getting other numbers when I press enter. I wonder if I'm getting the right outcomes or not.

Why's payroll so complicated?

At 4pm I try answering the phone. It's someone who can't get their password to work. Janet says they've only bought software for one computer while trying to install it in five. I tell them how much the multi-computer version costs. They call me the f-word and hang up.

So far so good.

I turn my phone off and pack up. That's enough for today.

Jim complains more about the noise from the builders on the way out. He tells me his neighbours yell all night too and it's starting to really stress him out.

I stop and listen hard and can hear the faint sound of a drill and men shouting. Jim must have really sensitive ears.

I shout goodbye to Janet and Chris. Maybe I'll get the hang of this whole payroll software thing tomorrow.

Tomorrow I don't get the hang of it.

The builders are louder today. They must be closer. Jim's bought noise cancellation headphones but says they don't do crap. Janet's dog's decided he likes me and has been rubbing his scabby bits on my polyester skirt until the static electricity makes sparks.

It's also Janet's birthday. She brings in doughnuts and wears a badge. It has LED lights and sings Happy Birthday and sounds like a depressed ferret on a kazoo. She invites everyone to the pub after work, but I can't go because I'm down to my last 50p and am living off free custard creams from the office kitchen.

Jim says he's going to call the police tonight if his neighbours are still yelling. He's getting really agitated with the noise. I've started to feel the same with the builders at work now. I can barely even hear the phone when it rings.

I decide to hide in the toilets.

There's no paper in the first two. The third door's kept closed. Nobody wants to look at the toilet on which Shane died. I think about opening it to see if it has paper, catch myself about to knock first and freeze. I wouldn't call myself a coward, I did after all start wearing cold shoulder tops before they started selling them in Primark, but that whole Japanese ghost toilet thing struck a chord. I don't want a dead Shane yelling at me.

The next day I come in and Janet and Chris are looking unhappy. The builders are using what sounds like a concrete mixer. I still can't see where their building site is but it's got to be a major deal.

Turns out, Jim isn't coming in today. Turns out Jim called the police last night on his neighbours. Only Jim doesn't have any neighbours.

Turns out Jim hears voices.

Karen's really nice and tells us not to worry about the phones today. She says something about Jim getting help and that if any of us feel stressed to talk to her.

I'm not going to talk to her. I've only had the job a few days. I can't afford to lose it. Instead I go home early and eat stolen custard creams while washing my underwear in the shower.

The next day everyone tries to get on like normal. This means more fannying about for me. I make a promise to myself that the minute I can afford the internet I'll Google payroll and try and learn what the hell any of this means. Jim still isn't in. He's getting help apparently and is expected back soon. It's probably best he stays away from here for a bit anyway. The builders are getting louder every day. I mention this to Janet and she looks at me strangely and pets her dog. Then I start to panic.

What if there are no builders?

I've not seen any builders.

Maybe I'm the only one who hears them. Maybe I've gone like Jim. I've got Blu Tack in my shoes, panty-liners in my armpits and I'm scared of a toilet. Maybe I even imagined Jim?

No. Calm down. Everybody's talking about Jim. I haven't made up Jim.

Chris asks us if we want coffee. I try and work out how I can ask if the builders are real without letting on that I can hear them. I'm all out of ideas. Then I come up with it.

Shane.

I could go down to the bathroom and knock.

If Shane answers, I've gone like Jim. If he doesn't, happy days.

My phone rings. I still have absolutely no clue what I'm doing but I'm going to answer it. Perhaps I should get a support animal. That dog of Janet's really seems to help.

I'll knock on the bathroom door tomorrow.

After all, I'm pretty tired today. Last night my neighbours kept me up with their fighting.

SILVER SANDS

Richard Lakin

Sun pokes through a gap in the curtains and wakes me. Something's buzzing; trapped in the nets. I paw at the curtains and wipe sleep from my eyes. A tumbler, cloudy with fingerprints, is in my eyeline. It reeks of last night's Scotch. I pad over to the sink, clearing the unwashed crocks to fill the kettle. When I get the gas lit, I tug on my joggers and the cleanest t-shirt I can find, before filling my flask with black coffee. I grab the carrier bag with my things in it and jump in the Corsa. Two or three months, that's what they said. I told them I'd need money. I told them I'd think about it. No, you won't, they said. You'll go tonight.

I change down into second and hug the drystone walls and high earth banks of the lane. Last thing I need is an accident and some nosy copper asking for my licence and insurance. I tuck into a lay-by as a farmer passes in a battered Land Rover, his sheepdog's ears flapping in the wind. The lane twists and turns and narrows, before the hawthorn breaks, giving way to the full sweep of Silver Sands, waves crashing on the ribbed shore. I take a gulp of the salty air and, for a moment, if I had a bucket and spade, I could be five again. The world is a small space these days, they said, so I'm careful. I take the spot nearest the exit. The Corsa isn't memorable, but there's a patch of rust on the driver's side wheel arch. Another week and I'll tape it, give it a respray. I jog to the top of a dune and survey all I can see. There's a kite-surfer, three guys beach-casting, half a dozen or so kids on bodyboards, and a couple of pensioners walking dogs. The shutters are still down on Mr Blue Sky, a beach café with the song's lyrics painted on its gable end.

Fitting in is key with a scam. I've got to be part of the scenery. I get changed behind the car: if you can call pulling on a fluorescent yellow tabard changing. It's going to be a scorcher, so I change into beach shorts too. After a quick glance about, I open the boot and take out the A-board, setting it down in front of the hut at the entrance to the car park. For a homemade effort I reckon I've made a decent enough job of it. I've used black marker and a stencil. It says parking is four quid, no concessions. It's not greedy and it is for a full day. I drag the school chair into position in the hut and grin as a VW Campervan pulls up, painted out like it's Scooby Doo.

'Gorgeous day,' the fella driving says.

'Nowhere better in the world when it's like this,' I reply.

Four pound coins rattle into the ice-cream tub. It's a steady stream of jeeps and cars and people carriers after that. Families trail down to the beach with armchairs, tables, barbecues and radios, kites and drones and picnic blankets. Some seem to be carrying the contents of their living rooms, as if they've transported a little piece of Stoke or Manchester to the sand dunes of Anglesey.

I stack the coins into neat piles and fold the notes, humming 'The King is in his counting house' as I reckon up. There's nearly 600 quid and it isn't yet midday. Silver Sands is an apt name. Maybe at last my luck's changing. I unlock the boot and pour the coins into the spare wheel, cushioning their giveaway rattle with old rags. I fold the notes in a plastic bag, zipping them into my shorts. I keep a few coins handy as a treat and buy a 99 flake for old times' sake.

I paddle at the shoreline, checking out a few of the mums. It's warm in the shallows and I kick and splash as I finish my ice cream, tossing the nibbled cone to a gull. I close my eyes and tilt my head back to catch the sun as I walk out into the toppling waves. I like the feel of the ribbed sand in the arches of my feet. A wave breaks and fizzes against my knees. It's at this moment I hear the screams.

A skinny little boy in orange shorts stands on a sandbank out in the bay. There are plenty of signs warning of the tide, but it seems no one reads them. He's balling his fists and pacing up and down, and when the wind changes direction it carries his crying. His mum runs down the beach in leggings and baggy t-shirt, stumbling in the loose sand. She keeps looking back at a toddler in bonnet and romper suit trotting away from their windbreak. I glance about for Dad, for anyone, but there's no sign. It's a huge bay and there's no one else this end of the beach. Lifeboat, I think, but I pat down my trunks and realise my phone's in the car.

'Help me, please. My boy's out there. Help me!'

I stop her running into the waves. I tell her to calm down, but she shrugs me off. I grip her wrists until she's forced to look at me. I tell her to phone the lifeboat, police, anyone. I strip my t-shirt off and get a few strides out when I remember the money. I turn my back to take the plastic bag from my shorts, folding it inside my t-shirt. I hand it to her.

'What're you playing at?'

She screams at me to move, to save him. I run into the surf till I'm waist deep, the tide sucking at my legs. A fast, deep channel cuts the sandbank off from the beach. The boy shouts something and jumps back as the water rises. I aim for the opposite end of the sandbank and kick hard, knowing the tide will drag me off course. I swallow and cough, my eyes streaming with salt water. He's waving his hands, but I can't hear as the waves crash over me. I scramble onto the sandbank on all fours, gasping, with ears full of water. I grab his tiny hand, but I can't speak. We're on a spit of sand that's being sliced by each wave. A few more minutes and we'll be knee-deep. Wet sand sucks at my knees as I drag myself up to stand. I make a cup of my palm and push it against my ears, till the water bleeds from them and I can hear him again.

'Over there,' the boy shouts.

I don't know how we're going to get back, but then I see what he's pointing at.

The lifeboat was on a training exercise in the next cove. They give us blankets, sweet tea, and a shelter from a sea breeze that now seems a biting wind. They take us into the harbour where Tommy's mother is waiting, waving from the quayside, strapping the little one into his pushchair, fiddling with her phone.

'Now I'm in for it,' the boy says.

'She got a fright, that's all.'

She flings her arms around him, then kisses me. 'You saved my Tommy.' She takes the t-shirt from her handbag. I clutch it, relieved to feel the plastic bag inside. I don't know if she's looked, but she says nothing. 'Come on, I'll get us coffee,' she says.

'Nah, it's all right.'

'You saved my boy's life.'

'They did that.' I nodded at the lifeboat crew.

'You must be starving. Tommy is, aren't you?' The boy grins. 'I'll get us coffee and bacon rolls.'

I see she won't be persuaded otherwise. 'Okay but first I got to, erm –' I gesture at the toilets behind Mr Blue Sky.

'Well don't be long,' she says.

I feel bad, but I've no choice. I watch them go inside and join the queue, then I sprint across the dunes to the car.

Tommy cries when the man doesn't come back. Donna's angry at first, thinking it's rude, but on reflection he seems the type of guy who hates a fuss. She takes out her phone and scrolls through it, zooming in on the shot she's got of him climbing out of the lifeboat. She uploads it to Twitter and Facebook. She posts: Can you help me find the guy who saved my Tommy's life? Soon, the replies are rolling in. She has reporters on the phone asking her to tell the full story. She's got him stripping and dashing into the waves. Buff he is too. It's not just the newspapers either. She has some guy from Birmingham who wants to know all about the hero in the sea. She doesn't think to get his name.

'I want to reward him,' he says. 'I've got something for him.'

THE GIRL ON THE SWING

Annest Gwilym

I was on the swing, kicking my legs into the cooling evening air, my sister tending to the snail collection she kept in an old shoe box, when Mum's car pulled up the drive. Nigel was with her, grinning at us from the passenger seat like a hairless chimpanzee.

We both pretended we hadn't seen him, faked concentration on what we were doing. I wanted to stick out my tongue, but I knew there'd be consequences, like having to go straight to bed after feeling the sting of the hairbrush on my bottom.

Out of the corner of my eye, I saw that Mum and Nigel were taking suitcases and boxes out of the boot.

'Girls, come and help us carry these indoors – Nigel's coming to live with us.'

Emily and I exchanged a quick glance – it was bad enough that he sometimes stayed overnight, but to come to live with us ...

We carried a box or two, full of his smelly old trainers and jackets that reeked of cigarette smoke.

I wished that I could speak to Dad about this, but he now had a new family with twin baby boys, Simon and Hugh, who we called Squealer and Howler. How he could prefer those stinky little piglets to us was beyond me – all they did was cry and fill their nappies. When they started screaming their skin turned the colour of boiled ham.

'Mandy, Ems, we'll have to go on a picnic to the beach tomorrow to celebrate,' said Mum.

I remembered the last time we went to the seaside with Nigel, at the beginning of the summer holidays. Emily and I had been making a sandcastle all afternoon, the biggest and best on the beach. It had a moat with seaweed in, and turrets decorated with delicate pink seashells which looked like ladies' nails with varnish on. We had even made a garden for it with cut up pieces of marram grass stuck in the sand, and those pretty pink and white flowers which grew in the sand dunes. On one of his many trips to the beach café, Nigel *accidentally* tripped and kicked it over, then laughed like a hyena.

'Castles always fall down,' he joked.

Emily started to cry, but I just stared hard at him, which made him laugh even more.

On the walk back to the car park we followed a river which emptied out into the bay. I went into it for a final dip – it was a very pretty blue colour because of some *mineral* in the earth, Mum said. Nigel had followed us in, always wanting to be at the centre of things.

Suddenly, I felt his big fat hand on top of my head, pushing it down. I panicked, flailing arms and legs, swallowing the foul estuary water. I started to feel a fizzing in my head, like it was full of cola, then he released his hand and I rose to the surface spluttering and crying.

'Mum, he was trying to drown me ...'

'Of course he wasn't, Amanda! And you're too big to be making a racket like that!'

Nigel had that nasty grin on his face. Emily was crying too by now, and we were quiet the whole way home. After tea, we went straight up to our bedrooms. I never wanted to go to that beach again.

In the evenings, after washing up the tea things, my mum always took out the vodka bottle from the fridge *to help her relax*. By our bedtime, she was usually flushed and starting to slur her words. If she ran out, Nigel got in the car to buy her more. We usually stayed away from Mum in the evenings, because she got cross with us so easily.

So after helping Nigel unpack, as usual, the bottle came out.

'Nigel, can you tuck the girls in? I'm tired,' she said.

This was new, and completely unwelcome.

'There you are, Mandy-Bear' he said, pulling the quilt over me. No one had ever called me such a stupid name before, not even my real Dad, so I scowled at him.

'This'll cheer you up,' he said as he laid his big fat body over me and started to tickle me around the ribs and belly with his nicotine-stained fingers. I couldn't move, and almost wet myself trying to wriggle free. Then it was suddenly over, he readjusted the quilt and muttered a soft 'Nighty-night' as if nothing had happened.

After that I heard him cross the landing to Emily's room. 'Emy-Baby' I heard him say as he entered the room. I knew she would hate that – she was always trying to be a *big girl* like me.

A quarter of an hour later a weeping Emily came into my room and crept into my bed, something she hadn't done since she was a tiny child afraid of the *monster* that lived in her wardrobe. We hugged and she slept curled up next to me.

The next day, Mum was grumpy as she usually was in the morning, pouring herself some *keep calm vodka* into her orange juice. Nigel sat there with his strong black coffee and a cigarette, flicking ash onto the red gingham tablecloth.

'Make your sandwiches, Mandy,' Mum said, pointing to the sliced white loaf and peanut butter on the working top. They were so dry that sometimes they stuck to the top of my mouth, making me gag. Sometimes, as a treat, she let me put jam in them, but her face was like thunder and I knew better than to ask today. Sometimes, my friend Sara would swap one of hers for mine, so I didn't have to eat the same lunch every day. Sara never came round to my house anymore – I'd lied to her that Mum didn't want visitors because she was ill.

Nigel was now buying my mum two bottles of vodka each day, instead of one, so she was usually drunk by the time we came home from school. She would still be in her nightdress and dressing gown, her hair a mess. She barely turned to look at us when we came in, and some loud game show would always be blaring on the telly.

When Nigel came home from work, he would sometimes make us a snack, or send us out for fish and chips or a pizza. Mum now only ate the packets of Doritos he bought her, or our leftovers.

In the evenings, I would try to get Nigel to go out at our bedtime, so he couldn't tuck us in.

'Nigel, I think Mum needs more vodka.'

But it didn't work, because he'd only come in later instead. Emily was becoming even quieter than usual; she never cried now or camc to sleep in my bed. Whenever Nigel came to visit me, I would squirm about and make so much noise that in the end he stopped coming, and only went in to see Emily.

'Why aren't you nice like your little sister, Mandy?'

Once I pretended to be scared of sleeping alone and slept on my quilt on Emily's floor, but that only got me into trouble with Mum.

'You ungrateful little bitch, I give you a room of your own and what do you do, sleep on Emily's floor!'

Emily started to get pale and thin, a bit like some of those poor children they always showed in Charles Dickens films at Christmas. She took the sandwiches I made for her lunch but just dumped them in a bin on the way to school. She wasn't talking much either, not even to me, who she always used to confide in. She never went out to play on the swing anymore, just stayed in her room playing with her dolls. I freed the snails from their shoe box because she wasn't feeding them any fresh grass or leaves.

Nigel was spending more and more time in Emily's room in the evenings. As long as she had her vodka, Mum didn't care. Nigel's nasty grin had gone, and he took no notice of me or Mum.

One night when Mum was dozing on the couch, mouth open and drooling, I sneaked into her handbag and took out her mobile phone. I crept upstairs as quietly as I could, stepping over the creaky stair, and stood outside Emily's room. I very carefully pushed the door slightly ajar and took a photo of Nigel on top of Emily with Mum's phone, his trousers on the floor. Then I tiptoed to my room and hid the phone in my school bag.

The next day, after the last lesson, I showed Mrs Wells the photo on the phone. Soon after, the police came to our house and took Nigel away. We never saw him again after that.

It would be a long time before Emily started speaking again.

RUNAWAY

Gillian Wallace

Without Brian, I'd have died that first winter. Ex-army, ex-Afghanistan, ex-everything, he says.

I warned him off when he came round to say hello, showed him the kitchen knife I'd pinched from Mum.

He smiled. 'Could you kill a bloke? Because that's the only way you'd stop most men.'

I pictured Steve's pig of a face. 'Yes. If I had to.'

Brian left me alone but he always spoke. I never answered but I suppose I got used to him being there.

Then he brought me a chip supper. I thought he'd stolen it, sure he'd want something in return and nearly threw it at him. But the smell made my stomach groan. I hadn't eaten for two days, apart from stale bread pinched from the pigeons in the square.

I opened the parcel after he disappeared next door, burnt my tongue, didn't care. It tasted fantastic.

I had to go and thank him, didn't I? Stood in front of his dirty beard as I jiggled from one tatty trainer to the other. He didn't say a word, just waited till I'd finished. I even apologised for accusing him of stealing, which I hadn't, not out loud anyway.

He nodded and closed his eyes. I was ready to run if he moved but he didn't.

We became friends by degrees. I don't know how I got the idea he had a family. He didn't say exactly, it was something about the way he treated me. Seemed to know, to have experienced maybe, the way kids behave.

'Come on, Scruff,' he said one day. 'I found a place they don't ask questions. But they do have things we need.'

Scruff was the name I'd told him. My dog's called that. At least, she was. Before Steve got rid of her. Mikey reckoned he'd tied a brick around her neck and chucked her in the canal. That was the last time I cried.

Brian took me through ginnels to the back of an old church. He knocked, the door opened and a voice said, 'Hi.'

I got closer to Brian than I ever had, scared of being separated, unsure of this place. We walked along a dark passage and into Aladdin's cave. It was magical. There were shelves from floor to ceiling filled with tins and other things, even personal stuff.

Brown eyes smiled at me below short blue hair. I stared for a moment. Couldn't see any sign of whiskers, so I settled on a she. I glanced across as Brian asked about her kids. That worried me, the fact this wasn't his first visit. What if, I thought? But I'd run out of sanitary towels and was fed up of being followed around Boots. Stealing wasn't difficult until they got that new security guard.

'You pick up what you need and I'll get the food. Okay?' Brian said as he handed me a wire basket.

I didn't take much, figured I'd come back later because I wanted out. I was scared they'd call the Social, or worse yet, the police.

We sat on a wall eating out-of-date sandwiches. Odd, isn't it? The way hunger almost makes me yearn for Mum's house, her kitchen cupboards stacked with ready meals, crisps and choccie biscuits. I could taste them through jellied cheese and pickle on shop-white bread.

It's history so I deleted it. Again.

'Dirty fucking beggars!'

It wasn't the words. It was the spittle landing on my food jerked me off my bum. I was going to punch the kid's face off.

I landed two good ones, right in the middle of his nose. He started squealing, so not tough at all, unlike Mikey who'd have thumped me good if he'd caught me.

Only there were three others, big, mean and beer-bellied. I backed away. They followed. To fight wasn't an option and flight several seconds too late. I shouldn't have stopped to enjoy my revenge because they were intent on shafting me, probably for real after a beating.

Brian caught my arm and swung me around behind him.

'Take the gear, Scruff. Run!'

I left my ruined lunch, lugged our rucksacks and ran for home. My shop doorway was the best of the row, deep in shadow most of the day. It kept the rain off and I could curl up and hide at the back. The postman never called, hadn't forever because a rusty metal plate covered the slot.

It was a while before Brian arrived. He sat down beside me and answered my question, sort of. 'Bullies give up when they're outclassed.'

'Three of them?'

'Ex-army, remember?'

He showed me how to defend myself, had me practise till I was sore and tired. Sometimes I didn't like him at all but we talked afterward. His stories were weird as I found it hard to imagine countries where women and kids died for no reason.

He's not nosy but I told him about Steve throwing me out of Mum's house after I had Mikey fix a lock on my bedroom door. I worry about Mikey which is why I never visit. Always thought he was Mum's pet, her favourite child, but I don't think she'll protect him. She's afraid of Steve too.

Brian taught me to be aware of who was around and the safe places to wash. He said the old church was run by the Sally Army, that I could trust them, they were good people and I should treat them the same.

One evening, he spoke about his time in the military, said it was his mates he missed the most.

'Couldn't settle when I left. I tried.' He shrugged. 'It's time to move out, Scruff. We need another bolthole.'

I didn't see why but went with him to look at the place he'd found. It was the other side of the old church, further from the town centre and not too far from a hostel.

'I'm not going in there,' I told him. 'It's for down and outs.'

He laughed. 'Like I said. Backup. Next winter could be a bad one. What d'you think?' he asked pointing at a double shop doorway.

'I suppose.'

I didn't fancy living so close even though I did trust him now.

'We can build a barrier, make each space more private?'

I nodded and we went for our belongings. It was another sunny day like when Steve arrived as Mum's lodger.

Brian swore, startling me. And the smell hit. Our things, what was left of them, were rotting in pee and worse.

Someone sniggered. Brian stopped mid flow and we faced the beer bellies again. Each held a baseball bat, one across his chest, the other two swinging them from meaty fists.

I didn't wait for Brian. Fury bit and fight was definitely better than flight. I jumped to reach the nearest. My fist thumped into his mouth and he went down. I grabbed his weapon off the tarmac, smashed it across his head as he tried to get up. He fell like a puppet with tangled strings.

'Scruff!'

I twisted away from a shadow, jabbed the bat hard into a fat belly and turned to help Brian.

Too late.

Blood followed the knife. Brian slipped sideways.

A grinning face swung my way and sunshine flashed from his blade.

Too much. Too much fear. I ran.

Didn't take long. I crouched against our new door, made myself small. Shivers took ages to settle. Thoughts of nothing and one person I daren't picture. I remembered the smell of blood, hadn't noticed before. He'd warned me to keep my temper. I hadn't.

Darkness threatened. The shakes returned. Must leave. This place isn't safe.

Not tonight. I looked at the tiny pile of belongings we'd brought with us, left Brian's rucksack till later. My sleeping bag was rolled up behind it. I just needed something extra to keep the cold out.

The local shop's skip wasn't far. I was in luck, there were old cardboard boxes as well as piles of newspapers. I scuttled back to the doorway as a street light lit up the entrance.

Couldn't sleep, even after saying sorry to Brian, so I took a paper to the light. I'd settled but my ears strained for footsteps.

A headline stated two people had died in a house fire in Welland Road. I wondered if I knew them but it's a long street. They weren't named and I lost interest.

I decided to ask the Sally Army woman about Brian. He might be in hospital and she'd know how to find him. That made me feel better.

Sleepy and a little cold, I rolled to my knees and twitched upright. The paper slipped off and slithered apart. Too tired to care, I shuffled the sheets together and noticed the picture I'd missed below the house fire article.

It was an old photo taken in the snow of Mum and Mikey.

WORMS ON THE PLAYGROUND

Anne Mackey

'It's about power,' Doug said. He shifted in his seat, took another mouthful of coffee and screwed up his eyes against the steam. 'Power and control. You have it, they take it away and you can't do nothing without it. Look at them refugees.' He motioned to the TV screen fixed to the wall opposite. 'Just living their lives. Doctors, lawyers some of them. In control, then wham, they have to get out and it all goes to shit.'

I could feel my interview sliding out of control. I consulted my list of questions to try and get us back on track.

'What got you to the class in the end, Doug?' I asked. I thought: how many times did you get to the door and turn away, ashamed? How many occasions when you 'forgot your glasses'? Or you picked up the dog food instead of the baked beans because the Basics range means all the cans look the same and you couldn't read the writing?

He didn't need to think about this.

'My grandson,' he said simply. 'We was at football training. They gave us all forms to fill in for a trip. I couldn't read it. No form – no trip. I thought – no, not this time.'

'So what stopped you learning at school?'

'I'm the same as you.' He nodded towards my hand; I was frantically making notes. 'Left handed. In my day they tied our left hands behind our backs. Teacher wrote on the blackboard and you copied it down. They'd rub it off before I was halfway through and start with another load of stuff. I just never caught up. So I stopped trying.' He smiled then, eyes crinkling over sunken cheeks. A face used to hardship. 'Hasn't stopped you, though. Here you are teaching us. Maybe things was different at your school?'

A sudden memory. St Gregory's Roman Catholic Infants and Juniors. It's 1963 and I am four years old.

A late heatwave means light and heat are hitting the playground hard. Everyone is playing except those of us in the reception class. It's our first day at school and we are unsure of what to do. We hover around the edges, looking on as the older children play hopscotch or tag or skip with plastic washing lines. There's a patch of dried mud interspersed with clumps of grass where some boys are kicking a ball around.

The tarmac surface of the playground has several small ridges which are puzzling us. Claire steps out bravely from the edge and reports back: they are worms, trying to cross. On one side sun-hardened grass offers no shelter from the heat. On the other, the cool, welcoming dampness in the shadow of the school building offers a place of safety. In between, a sea of hot tarmac, noise and confusion to be faced down.

Most don't make it. Timing is everything. Linger too long on this ocean of hot, undulating grey and their bodies dry out. Eventually fate takes its course.

Our instincts tell us to rescue those we can, but we have had a bewildering morning and our certainties about what we are allowed to do have been whipped away from us, leaving us almost paralysed.

The day starts well. Nervous, excited, we cling to our mothers' dresses as we arrive at the school entrance. New, home-sewn school uniforms, Start-Rite brown lace-up shoes, wonky home-cut fringes. Claire was five three days ago; as I am still four, she has been instructed to look after me. Everyone knows the Big Ones look after the Little Ones. Mothers and small brothers and sisters wave cheerful goodbyes and we are led into school by Miss Flinn, tall and thin with hair the colour of steel.

The classroom has windows so high we cannot see out. The wall opposite the blackboard has the letters of the alphabet pinned up, with a picture alongside each. Underneath the windows, statues of the Holy Family face the door. Claire and I are seated together. We are told to sit up straight and to fold our arms. Miss Flinn calls out names and tells us to say 'Yes, Miss,' when we hear ours.

When she has finished, she takes a stick and taps the first of the letters.

'A is for Apple' Miss Flinn says. 'Repeat.' We do, through to Z is for Zebra. Claire slides a look at me. We've been doing this for weeks at home. We relax very slightly.

Next, we are going to do some writing. Miss Flinn writes on the blackboard: Thursday 5th September.

'Who knows what this says?' she asks. We do. We call out simultaneously.

'No, little girls.' Miss Flinn says sharply. 'If you know the answer, you put your hand up. Like this.' She demonstrates. 'If you shout out again you will have to stand in the corner.'

We are silent. Apparently standing in the corner is a bad thing.

We are each given an exercise book. Miss Flinn writes letters on the board.

'Write each letter five times,' she instructs. Again, we can do this. Our mothers have taught us to write our alphabet. We begin.

Miss Flinn begins a slow tread around the room, padding quietly, looking at what each child is doing. Those children who have never picked up a pen look scared as she gets close to them. When she looms over me I am not worried. I know how to do this. I think she must like my letters, drawn carefully and with precision.

But no. She bends over and plucks the pencil out of my left hand and pushes it into my right.

'Not that hand,' she says. 'You use your right hand to write with. Start again.'

I am instantly rendered helpless. What I found so easy is now impossible. I try. I make some squiggles. I look at Claire in confusion. Her face reflects my distress.

There is a disruption. Miss Flinn has smelt something untoward in the classroom. Thirty nervous children at school for the first time has produced an inevitable outcome.

Miss Flinn stands at the front of the class. 'Someone has filled their pants,' she says. 'Stand up, please, whoever it is.'

No one moves.

'Very well,' she says. 'You will form a line outside the toilets and I will check each of you until I find the child responsible.'

Ahead of me in the queue a small girl cries silently, tears pouring down her cheeks. Even though I am upset about no longer being able to write, I can sense how awful it must be as we draw nearer and nearer to Miss

Flinn and the toilet cubicle. Eventually the culprit is discovered and handed over to the school nurse in disgrace.

The delay takes us to break time, and the worms. We are to continue with our writing when we return to the classroom. The minutes tick away until the bell rings and we file back inside. Reluctantly, I sit down on my chair and try again. I can barely make a mark on the paper. Miss Flinn resumes her padding. I can sense Claire twitching in her seat alongside me; she takes her caring responsibilities seriously.

Miss Flinn gets nearer. Large teardrops fall onto the paper as I give in to my distress. She stops next to me. She looks. She opens her mouth to speak.

Then, a furious voice. Blue eyes blazing, and hand definitely not up, Claire twists around in her chair and glares up at Miss Flinn. She shouts at her:

'You shouldn't make her write with that hand! She can't write with that hand!'

The universe grinds to a sudden halt.

Above the clouds, the gods pause in their deliberations.

Twenty-eight pairs of eyes look up, stricken, as each child wonders what Miss Flinn will do next.

What Miss Flinn does next is – nothing. She looks at Claire's angry face. She looks at me. She deliberates. She walks on.

The universe lets out its breath, slowly.

Claire pulls the pen from my right hand and I grab it with my left. I write all the letters, five times each. The bell rings for dinner time.

At 3.30pm our mums are outside the entrance to Reception with prams and pushchairs. Everyone is talking, hugging, laughing, consoling. Our first day is over.

Claire and I look at each other. Then we slip away around the corner to the playground.

On the still-hot tarmac, more worms are making their perilous journey. Claire marches to the other end; I stay where I am. Then we work our way towards each other, picking up each worm in turn and carrying it to safety.

The rattle of grinding coffee beans brought me back to myself. Doug was looking at me curiously.

'Was it then?' he asked. 'Different, I mean?'

I smiled at Doug. I made a mental note to call Claire at the weekend.

'Yes,' I said. 'I was lucky.'

PASSED WIGAN SOMEWHERE

John Minshull

Is it possible to be bored and fall at 120mph at the same time? Or is bored even the right world to describe being distracted by radon thoughts whilst you're plunging to your death? And why, even though I'm a metric kid does 120mph sound so much cooler than 193kph? I suppose nearly 200kph sounds pretty cool, but even though we're all metric kids now, we're still five foot six tall, we weigh nine stone, and I even saw Miss Edwards sneaking looks at her ruler when she was explaining that her grass was at least 15cm tall when she got back from her singles' holiday in Marrakech. She must be easily 35, so you think shed know how Europe measures things by now. Personally, I don't think she has a clue. Aaron thinks she's a babe; I reckon he just needs a stronger prescription.

I guess I ought to explain, before you think I'm a total dork, that what you're reading is me talking to my VoyceRec software, and I haven't got time to go back and do all the edits, so you'll have to live with the miss takes. Just believe me when I say I don't have much time left at the moment. That's not because I really am plunging to my death ... that was last week. And I didn't die. I was using up the voucher Uncle Bran gave me as a birthday percent. Tandem skydiving. Defying death whilst strapped to Kevin the accountant. You're supposed to be 16 to do it, and even though I'll be there next year, you know I still look stupidly young. It wasn't a problem, though, I just nudged his purple a little bit, and he signed the form and went straight into 'cool hero' mode (if canopy malfunctions and exit procedures can ever be cool). To be fair, I suppose board isn't quite the right word for the ride down; the view was nice, and I got a bit of a rush from the fist acceleration, but once we got to TV (that's terminal velocity BTW, and even though you can't see it, I'm holding my face just like Kevin did when he said it) things settled down a bit, and I started to get distracted.

I'm not like other kids. I know, I know, every fifteen-year-old in history has said that, and I also know that some of you have some pretty weird secrets, but you're my classmates, and I suppose I've got to know you guys a lot over the last couple of years, sew I wanted you to understand, before I leave. It's sort of like that 'Sunscreen' track that was out a few years back. You know, thee American college teacher who was saying goodby to all the graduates (it's called a valedictory speech, in case you wondered, and I'm wondering if VoyceRec even knows that word). Anyway, the point is, he was saying to the kids ... or whatever you call someone between kid and adult ... that they should listen to his advice on things heed got wrong, then they wooden have to make the same mistakes again, so love your Mom and Dad, and trust me on the sunscreen etcetera ... you get the picture. That's what I want to do for you, sort of leaf you something to remember me by.

It doesn't matter how, or why I'm different, just take my word for it. Just as an example, though, that bit at the beginning where I said I had to push Kevin's purple a bit to get him to sign the form, that wasn't a VoyceRec mistake, it's what I actually said. I can see people's auras, and though the phonies say auras are about health or spirit, or some other pigpoo, they're not. They are an extension of what's going on in your brian, so if you're working on a maths problem, you might push out some yellow, or a boring lesson might be green (and Lainey, you were really lit-up in maths last week!). Sometimes, I peek around my parents' door at night just to see the lightshow my Dad puts on when he's dreaming, it's really awesome. Kevin the hero was doubting I was sixteen, and that was coming out purple, so I just pushed it back in (you do that by thinking it, but that's too long a story for now) and Kevin had a sudden change of mined.

What I want you to do is see things a little differently. Believe me, it will help in ways you have no idea about. I was talking to that guy in Y13 with the ripped blazer and snotty sleeve the other day, and he was trying to describe where his Dad was working (he's not working away, by the way, he's in prison, but I'm trusting you not to blab that). He couldn't think what the town was, but he knew it was 'passed Wigan somewhere'. His view of the world was so tiny, I felt really sorry for him, and that's when I decided to leave you my little present. Time's short, so I've had to send this by email, but I don't want anyone else to find my gift to you, so I've buried it. You will be able to find it easily, but even if you don't, it will dissolve in a couple of weeks, and anyway, it's useless unless you know what to do with it.

I'll give you the instructions in a second, but first, here's a short description of what the gift is. It's actually a mind-control crystal. Don't worry though, it's not the evil Doctor Doom type, it's really, really good for you. Remember the auras, and how they are a sort of lightshow of what's going on in your brain? Well, this will modify your thought processes just a little bit, but the effects will last for the rest of your life. You'll see possibilities that other people can't, you'll be able to solve complicated problems, and languages will come easily to you. You'll find confidence to do things that you find difficult and you will also handle stressful situations more easily. The more you use this gift, the more useful it will become, and you'll use it to help other people too. I'm not going to say too much about how to use it, because you'll find your own weigh, and you'll all use it differently anyway. Whatever you do though, this is my gift to each of you individually, and I hope it will also bind you together as a group forever in memory of the great times we had. Oh, one final thing ... probably best if you don't tell anyone outside our group about this, EVEN your parents. I've been pretty serious about these last few comments, because it's a serious topic, and seriously guys, I'm not joking, this is genuine, and genuinely the best thing that will happen to you, ever. Try it before you decide not to believe me.

As I'm not from this area, I was struggling to find a place to hide it, but I eventually decided it would be best where we had that great Boys v. Girls football match last summer. It's near the building that's got the same name as our Geography teacher and directly opposite the tree where Ches snogged Abi. Walk between the building and tree, and the crystal is buried in a cardboard box near the post of the dog-doo bin. Now, follow these instructions exactly. Find somewhere dark where you can all be together, and not be disturbed. Doesn't matter where, that's up to you, but indoors is probably best, and drawer the curtains, because there'll be a bit of light. Put the crystal where it can't fall over – an egg box might be good – then to activate it, you'll need a high voltage, and here's where your physics lessons come in. You need a high voltage, but practically no current, so take Matty's plastic ruler (the teddy bear one that we always teased him about) and Chrissie's rabbit fur pencil case, rub the ruler hard with the fur for about twenty seconds to generate static electricity, then touch it immediately on the crystal. Might be best to wear a rubber glove, two, to avoid any charge being lost through your hand.

When you've done this, the static charge will activate the crystal, and it will start to glow. Don't, under any circumstances, take your eyes off it, and try to blink as little as possible. The hole process will take around half a minute, and the effects will start pretty much straight away. After that, it's up to you, and I hope that when you experience the effects, you'll remember the great times we had.

I've got to go now, we're being picked up soon. Our place is almost a light-year away, so whilst it's not a mega-journey, it's far enough, but as I said, I'm not from around here.

THE PRIME MINISTER AT FIFTEEN

Sheona Lamont

There's nothing fair about life. People say that we're all equal, but we aren't. Like Martin, the boy I sat next to in science when I was twelve. He got leukaemia. They gave him drugs that made him sick and told him that he was cured, but he wasn't. Then they gave him a bone marrow transplant and more drugs. For a while he was fat and bloated then he was thin and sad looking but all that pain didn't save him. We said goodbye when school broke up for Easter, he didn't come back. There was no announcement. Our headmaster wasn't into all that mass hysteria and communal grieving that was popular at the time. I think he just didn't want to pay for the counselling that you had to provide for all the wailing kids. When we came back from the holidays Martin just wasn't there, his social media stopped being updated, it was as if he'd disappeared, I suppose he had really. I had to ask to be sure that he had died, you don't like to go round telling people about something like that unless you're absolutely sure.

I've been to his grave a few times to say hello, to say I'm sorry that he isn't going to have the life that the rest of us are going to have. You know, like nights out with the lads when we can drink legally rather than in my mate's garage. He won't have education, work, a family and such. The inscription on the grave said, 'Taken by God.' What a load of bollocks. If there is an all-powerful God she's a vindictive bitch, but then a lot of the girls I know are like that. How on earth can people think that there's a powerful and merciful God if she lets shit like that happen? And if she can't stop it then she's not all-powerful is she? It's not really worth being God if you're not all-powerful. Martin hadn't hurt anybody and next thing he's dead. What the hell is fair about that?

I really knew that life isn't fair when I saw all the big houses on the other side of town. How can we all be equal when I'm born into a family where my dad spends his giro at Wetherspoons lining up his first pint at half ten in the morning and someone else is born into a family with a big house and shitloads of money? They get sent to private school and I go to the comprehensive with my backside hanging out of a third-hand pair of pants from George at Asda. But don't get me wrong, I'm still lucky, I could have been born in a shithole in Africa. My Mam hit me when I said that and told me to mind my mouth because that's where we came from. It seems that only Presidents are allowed to call places shitholes. But it's true, millions of people don't have their own bog, they just dig a hole in the ground and shit in it. So the President's speaking the truth calling places shitholes but people are going mad about it. Seems to me that some people don't like to hear the truth and try to deny it. Bloody stupid if you ask me, denying the truth because it doesn't fit with your view of the world.

It's like when Aunty M comes round, I said she smells and my Mam hit me but she does smell. And she keeps bringing nits into the house because her kids have always got them. They're got ringworm too. She's always coming round on the cadge but really she's come round to nick something. She says she needs to borrow but she never brings anything back, she either breaks it or takes it to the pawn shop so it's stealing really, taking under false pretences. Well, that's what the Dibble said when we persuaded young Lenny to let us use his bike then left it in the park. It was gone by the time we told him where it was, someone else had nicked it. His dad didn't half go mad, swore that he'd take his belt to us but with all the fags he smokes he couldn't catch us, we left him coughing his guts up at the street corner.

At school they asked me what I want to be when I grow up. I said I would be a politician so I can sort out the difference between those who have a lot and those who have nothing. They seemed pleased with that, they liked the idea of taking from the rich to give to the poor, a bit like a political Robin Hood. It just shows how stupid some teachers can be. If you take from the rich and give to the poor then the rich will just stop working and no one will have anything so there has to be another way to equal things up, I just haven't worked out what it is yet. But politics is a good job, you see only half of the politicians have to work. They're the ones that run the country. The other half sit on the other side of parliament and shout abuse and take the piss out of the ones who are running the country and tell them they're getting it all wrong. Neat eh?

And did I say being a politician pays well? Yeah, I've checked on Google. You gets lots of expenses too so you can buy a flat in London as well as your place at home. When the Tories retire they all become merchant bankers and sit on boards, but I don't think it's like the boards carpenters use. But the Tories are amateurs compared to the Socialists. I'd have to be a Socialist because I want to sort out inequality but that's good because they make the most money. I've seen it on the tinterweb though they say a lot on the tinterweb is lies. Why would people do that, why do people tell so many lies? Anyway a bloke called Kinnock was a Socialist and he got at least ten million quid in wages and pensions even though he was only ever taking the piss. If you get to run the country you get even more. My parents say that a bloke called Blair was a big cheese when I was a baby. They said that he made an absolute dog's bollocks of running the country causing wars and people dying and stuff but he's worth at least fifty million quid now. In the States where they make all the telly and films their Socialists make even more. Billy Clinton didn't make as big a mess of running his country as Blair did here though the tinterweb says he did mess up some girl's dress. Well he and his wife are worth two hundred million dollars. And there was a bloke called Chavez in Venezuela who was so bad at running his country he virtually bankrupted it by giving tons of money away. Poor bloke died of cancer but they say his daughter's worth three billion dollars so the more you make a bollocks of your country the more cash you get, weird eh?

I want to stay on at school and do A levels. At GCSE I've learned about tons of places and how lots of people live and we're not all the same and we're not all born equal except that we all have one chance at life and I'm going to make the best of my chance so I don't end up sitting in Wetherspoons at half ten in the morning with a pint of lager and a newspaper with more pictures of tits than news. English A level would be good so I can talk right when I meet all those boffins at university. Then I'll learn more than I can just playing football on the rec each evening and picking up a giro each week like my Dad and most of my mates' dads. It's really sad that my Mam and Dad have nothing to look forward to but a packet of fags and the bottom of a glass but then my Dad says he can get the same for sitting on his backside as he can for working so he would be stupid to work wouldn't he? But if nobody worked then there would be no one to pay for the giros would there? And the tech teacher says that all the computers are made in China so unless I get educated I'll never get a job because everything's going to be made in China and we won't have any factories left. That's why I want to stay on at school even though most of the lads from our estate leave at sixteen. Stands to reason dunnit?

LEAVING THE ISLAND

Christine Ryan

The Zodiac waited, buffeted by wind and waves. Alex held the rubberised craft steady by slowly motoring around in a circle. He couldn't bring it in to the landing stage until someone was there to catch the line. Four guests had opted to walk the five kilometres over the island from the Lighthouse to reach this point. This had meant that he had had to make only one trip to the mainland with the others and all the luggage.

It had been difficult getting the other guests on board. The waves were high today and had been washing over the small wooden quay with some ferocity. There had been only two minutes between each wave to bring the Zodiac alongside and load up. The passengers were warned to be ready and move quickly. They were nervous and some needed a little persuasion to make the dash between the waves. It would be even more difficult here.

He scanned the rocky promontory. The sky was darkening; rain threatened. He hoped they wouldn't be long. Then he spotted them. The Belgian couple first, with Theo waiting for his wife every few steps, offering a helping hand where necessary, but she was moving quite quickly. Then the British ladies; the one in a pink anorak, nimbly skipping along, but looking back and calling to her friend who was also making good progress but was turning back and waving to the person in the distance. Someone in a long, black waterproof which was flapping in the wind like a cloak, giving a bird-like appearance.

This last one wasn't walking well, clutching a long pole and limping.

Theo had reached the landing stage; Alex brought the Zodiac alongside. He threw the line and hoped Theo would know how to wrap it around the small, wooden bollard. He hadn't thought to check if any of them would know what to do, but he was lucky. Theo caught the line and gave it a few loops around the bollard and threw it back to him with practised ease.

'Well done,' Alex called, and held the Zodiac steady as Theo helped his wife over the side. She looked relieved to be on board and sat down as he handed her a life jacket.

'Let's hope we get back before it pours,' she shouted cheerfully. Alex nodded, and held out a hand to the next guest clambering on board; the one in the pink anorak. He wished he could remember their names but with a turnover every few days it was impossible. She was breathing quite heavily, took the life jacket from him with a grateful smile and slipped it on. Her friend jumped on board easily and Alex looked to help the last one, the one in the long, black coat. His hand was ready to help but there was no one there.

'Off we go then,' shouted Theo as he jumped in and expertly unwound the line holding them steady.

'Better have a life jacket,' Alex called and tossed one to him while still looking quizzically towards the shore. 'All ready and correct?' he said automatically. No one else was looking towards the shore. Then he saw her, slowly drifting back along the uneven, stony track, using the pole and holding her hood over her face as the rain started in earnest. He looked at the guests, 'Just the four of you, then?' They looked back at him with frowns on their faces.

'Did you want us to bring the black fox too?' called Theo, chuckling. 'She certainly wanted to stay with us. And she tried to lead us astray by digging up the marker poles and running off with them!'

The British ladies glanced at each other.

'We didn't see her this time, but more of the marker poles are missing, we could hardly follow the path. It was a good job that Rachel didn't try to walk with her bruised foot, the ground is so uneven,' one of them murmured.

Alex concentrated on keeping the Zodiac in a straight line; he wanted to get his passengers to shore before the storm broke. He also wanted to check that Rachel was safe with the others. He remembered now; she was the one who had looked fit and healthy, but had not got into the boat easily when he had collected them two days ago. She had commented on white knuckle rides as she had gripped the hand holds and tried to hold her hood up without letting go too often. The others had joked about her not enjoying the thrill of the ride. But she had been knowledgeable about the tides and the wave strength, and was muttering about the life jackets being flimsy. Later that evening she had been particularly interested in the history of the island, this rocky outcrop just off Newfoundland.

The story that he always told was about the French countess who had been abandoned here, left by her sea captain husband, with her maid and the young man suspected of being her lover. The story had long intrigued him.

As he walked the tracks on the island checking that they were safe for the guests who came for a few days to experience the wild scenery and see whales close to shore, he had always looked for the cave where it was said they had sheltered. The cave where it was said that she had given birth to her love child. Where that child had died and had been buried by the maid. And where she was found alone, in a state of despair months later, weak from hunger and almost deranged. It had also been said that black wolves had been seen encircling the cave protecting her. A fanciful tale, but one that had always amused the guests, especially those who stayed in the small cottage quite a long walk from the Lighthouse which housed most of the guests and where meals were served. Walking back at night with torches in the inevitable wild weather made everyone a little nervous.

Wolves didn't live here, but a black fox had been seen this time. He thought it had some young cubs hidden somewhere. He remembered that it was Rachel who had managed to take a photo of it with her smartphone. She had been walking more slowly than the others staying in the cottage, and the fox had come close. She said it had dug up a marker pole as she watched and then run back and forth with it as if urging her to follow. Her photograph had shown it clearly, its green eyes bright in the gloom. They had all been envious.

Alex concentrated on getting the craft safely to the mainland. The wind was blowing in their faces as they bucked through the waves. This was really a white knuckle ride. He could see a small group of people waiting near where they would land. One, detached from the group, was moving towards the water's edge, the long black waterproof billowing out as if forming wings. One hand waved while the other pulled the hood closer.

'That must be Rachel,' he muttered to himself.

As they came along the jetty a little cheer went up. Everyone was glad that Alex had brought their friends safely from the island. The two British ladies clambered out and walked towards their friend who had been taking photos since the Zodiac had come into view and was keen to show them how dramatic it had looked.

Alex was puzzled. He looked for the black clad figure but there was no one else on the shoreline. He shook his head and concentrated on helping the guests retrieve their luggage. All he wanted to do now was return to the island and follow the path from the Lighthouse once more. He would follow the black fox and try to make sense of what he had seen today. This was going to make one more story to tell about the island of Quirpon.

A SEA CHANGE

Linden Sweeney

Nothing of him that doth fade,
But doth suffer a sea-change
Into something rich and strange.
(Shakespeare, *The Tempest*, Act 1 Scene 2)

'Well, this is something,' thought David, exhilarated by the sharp sea air and the squalling of gulls in the harbour. Holding onto the rope in the sea wall, he followed Judith down the steep steps from the quay to one of the many small boats that took visitors to the Farne Islands and back. It was basic with only a wheelhouse and green planks across and around the boat for seating. There was no cover and no toilet, as Judith had hoped there would be.

'Oh, there'll be trouble about that,' he thought, 'she won't be happy.' Judith sat down, and David had to take off his backpack to squeeze in next to her. They were sitting towards the back of the boat with two rows of people in front of them behind the wheelhouse. There must have been about fifty people squashed onto the small boat and there was a buzz of excitement as they waited for the engines to start.

'There's no toilet,' hissed Judith, 'you said there would be. The journey is going to take half an hour each way and then there's an hour and a half on the island. I don't know if I can last that long. I wish I hadn't had that second cup of tea now. In fact, I wish I hadn't agreed to this whole thing.'

David sighed, 'You'll be fine, love. Just don't think about it.'

'Well, that's easy for you to say. You don't have my bladder, do you? I wish I hadn't come. I don't even like birds.'

At that moment the boat's engine throttled up and they set off to Staple Island, the furthest of the Farnes. David smiled as he watched an arctic tern dive-bombing a fish. Far ahead he could see the shapes of the islands and his heart lifted. He had wanted to come out here and photograph the nesting puffins for such a long time. In previous years there had always been other priorities in May and June. Mainly Judith's, of course: a flower show or a summer concert. But finally, it was his turn, and he could feel the excitement in his stomach. He wondered how many puffins he would see and how close he would be able to get. His fingers ran around the ridged surface of his zoom lens in anticipation. He should be able to get some really good close-ups.

As they left the harbour there was quite a swell as the boat picked up speed. They were all buffeted by the wind and found themselves almost lifting in their seats at the top of the waves and then sitting down with a bump. David could taste the salt on his lips.

'This is quite exciting, isn't it?' David smiled at Judith.

'I am sure it is for you, but my stomach is turning.' She pulled a very unattractive retching face.

David turned his head away and noticed a couple sitting in front of him. They were holding hands, smiling at each other and laughing as the boat bounced up and down. They were both immaculately, but appropriately, dressed in smart jerseys, one pink, one blue, and both wore expensive waterproof jackets. They had fashionably groomed beards and well-cut hair and smooth, tanned skin. He thought he could see the glint of a stud earring. They looked so happy and beautiful.

David looked down at his own trustworthy, but worn, grey walking trousers. He then looked sideways at Judith who was busy changing from her trainers into her walking boots for landing. As she changed her socks, he noticed her feet. They were yellow and covered in hard skin. Her toenails were grey and flaky. He felt disgust rise in his throat. He imagined the feet of the young man in pink in front of him. His feet would be soft and perfectly pedicured with pink shell-like nails. They would be tanned and there might be dark curly hairs. David wondered what a pedicure would feel like. He imagined his toes being gently massaged.

He realised that Judith had become fat lately and wondered when she had stopped taking care of herself or if she ever really had. He couldn't remember ever really finding her attractive. Her clothes were baggy to cover her stomach and her trousers were too short. She cut her own hair and it showed.

'Oh, the smell! I think I'm going to be sick!' exclaimed Judith.

It was true that as they approached the island there was a very strong smell of rotten fish and guano. Unsurprising because the sheer towering cliffs ahead of them were covered in thousands of birds, all tucked into nests on the cliff face which was white with bird droppings.

'Those are all guillemots,' David exclaimed. 'Look, you can see the chicks.'

'I thought you dragged me here to see puffins,' said Judith. David ignored her complaint.

'The puffins will be nesting on the island itself, but look around. There are loads of them flying in, with fish in their mouths. You can see their orange legs dangling.' He wanted to stand up and take a picture but there wasn't room as Judith was bent double tying her boot laces.

'Look over there, those little black and white ones are razorbills,' he told her.

But she just turned away uninterestedly. David noticed that the couple opposite were pointing out birds to each other excitedly, taking turns to hold each other's bags so one could stand up and take pictures of the birds on the cliffs. David was surprised to find he was feeling rather jealous.

As they came towards the land, the swell was still quite heavy, making tying up tricky. As they clambered off the boat there was a member of the crew there to hand everyone up to a volunteer on the island who helped you onto the seaweed-covered stone jetty. Judith disembarked ahead of him and made quite a fuss about the boat going up and down and was quite bad-tempered about having to be heaved up onto the landing area. David was holding Judith's bag and his own, as well as his camera, but he stepped up easily and turned to see the young couple helping each other, holding one another's bags as each one stepped off the boat. They were so gallant and so appreciative of the crew's help that it made David smile.

Climbing up the steep path, his heart leapt as he saw puffins all around him. They were everywhere from three feet in front of him to as far as the eye could see. The air was thick with them too. He had dreamed about being here but this far exceeded anything he could have hoped for. Judith, however, was standing beside him, huffing.

'Are you just going to stay here the whole time and take pictures?' she asked.

'Yes, that was the idea.'

'Well, I will go and have a walk and see if I can find somewhere to sit and have my sandwiches. I daren't drink the tea in the flask of course. Maybe the smell will be better on the other side of the island.'

'Okay, but be sure to be back at the landing stage at 12.30.'

In the prevailing peace, amidst the shrieking of the birds, David just heard the silence. He stood for a while feeling the wind on his face, looking up to the sky, watching thousands of birds flying free, living their lives as they were meant to. He felt puffins flying so low above his head that he imagined he could feel their feathers gently ruffling his hair. One landed right in front of him with his orange beak full of silver sand eels. It seemed to stand and wait for David to take its picture. The sad clown-eyes looked straight at him, taking him in. It felt a bit like looking in a mirror. He saw a slightly comical, plump figure but one that could fly wherever he wanted. David felt, at that moment, perfectly happy. Life seemed suddenly so full of possibility.

At twelve o'clock, David stepped down onto one of the waiting boats that would take him back to Seahouses. He hugged his camera to him joyfully, looking forward to seeing what he had captured. There was space, this time, for him to take some shots of the puffins flying out to sea.

At Seahouses, he walked up the quay, back to his car. He sat for a while in the driver's seat looking out at the Farne Islands on the horizon. He looked at the clock on the dashboard: 12.30.

'She'll be wondering where I am,' he smiled as he started the engine and wondered at all that lay ahead of him.

AFTERWARDS

Jocelyn Kaye

So little time left with him. Javier lies in bed in a post-coital coma. I wonder briefly how he can be so relaxed when I'm in such turmoil, but then he doesn't know that it's our last time together, that it's over. Not yet. I watch the curve of his upper arm gently rise and fall in time to his breathing which escapes from slightly parted lips and try not to notice how young he looks. His tangled blond hair on the pillow is at odds with the dark stubble on his face and the stripe of hair that runs down his stomach and disappears under the covers.

I am married to somebody else.

Maybe Alex would forgive me my lapse. I'm too useful, surely? To run the home, sort our teenage sons out, all those sorts of things. But I'm kidding myself. Infidelity of any kind is and always will be a deal breaker.

I feel suddenly stifled by the hotel room that's hot with the smell of bodies, and kettle steam. I take a sip of tea, made with the complimentary tea bag that manages to be both bitter and weak at the same time. The string hangs over the side of the cup and I feel like a cat with a mouse dangling out of its mouth. The tea hasn't any milk in it; I can't bear the thick greasy taste of UHT. Javier always laughs at my English tea habit, and said he'd ring room service to bring up a glass of milk that I could use. Afterwards. But afterwards, of course, he fell asleep and I couldn't wait. I had to have tea now, hence I'm drinking it black, which I am not enjoying. Such is life.

When I signed up for Spanish evening classes, I was looking for a hobby, not a lover. The attraction between us was as immediate and intense as it was unexpected, and my world suddenly turned on a different axis.

I'd never been unfaithful before, not with anyone. I told myself that this strange new attention and flirting should be enough to satisfy my curiosity, as Javier's eyes locked with mine whilst teaching us gendered nouns. But it wasn't. After a few weeks I stayed behind after class, ostensibly to discuss homework. I consoled myself that kissing wasn't actually cheating, as Javier made his move and I let myself respond.

I'd always imagined that, having got used to someone's way of kissing over the years, it would feel extremely strange to kiss somebody else – different speed, different texture, different taste. And it did feel strange, in a way, to kiss Javier. But I liked the strangeness, a lot. I was on fire with it, I craved it. I wanted more, and when it went further, that felt strange and wonderful too. *Stop it now,* my sensible side cautioned, *before it gets out of hand.*

But I didn't stop it and it is now way out of hand. I think I love Javier. But it's not like when I first met Alex, when I floated in a silky bubble for two years, until the boys and Real Life came along to pop it and send me crashing to earth with a bang. Javier makes me feel as though I have a split personality: dizzy and high when I'm with him, dark, tired and miserable when I'm not. Like the morning after a whisky binge, I tell myself this is no good for me and promise myself I won't do it again. But then I'm checking my mobile and email, panicking if I don't hear back from him quickly enough, yearning for my next fix of him.

Javier hasn't asked me to leave Alex yet, and I look for signs that he loves me too, that I'm not risking everything for someone who doesn't even care. I know that he plans to go back to Madrid one day and he told me that I'd love it there. He said he wanted to show me everything in the city: The Plaza Mayor, the Royal Palace and take me to see his beloved *Los Blancos* ...

But this can't go on. Afterwards, I'm going to tell Javier that I'm ending this thing, us; that I want it to be over. I do want this to be over, not because I don't want him anymore, but because I am exhausted with wanting him, thinking about him until I can't think any longer. I'm tired of feeling guilty, immoral, selfish. I have conversations with Alex and the boys, yet I'm only half listening because I'm thinking about Javier and the way his hair curls around the bottom of his neck, the way he pronounces certain words. There only has to be a mention of Spain on the TV and my heart lurches ridiculously and I catch my breath. I worry that Alex will notice, but no. Not yet.

I had planned to tell Javier before, when I arrived at the hotel. Our hotel now. You see, even illicit lovers start to build a shared history, given time. Making my way up to the room, a rehearsed speech replayed on my brain. Since I met Javier, I've had to rethink my own language. I choose every word carefully and think about what I say in case some nuance that I take for granted is lost on him and means something other than what I want it to mean. But, sure of my words, I felt clear-headed and light, almost euphoric with the thought of my own goodness. Soon I would no longer be a cheat and a liar, but a decent person.

'Hola!' Javier answered my knock and I felt a stab at his shy grin and the delight in his face. I could feel my strength ebbing away now he was before me and I clenched my teeth and began to hate myself for weakening. I sat on the bed staring at the white sheet, twisting it hard with sweating fingers to keep my hands from shaking. I groped in my mind for my speech: words and phrases whirling round my brain, refusing to be tied down, controlled or spoken.

'Javier ...' I dragged my gaze to meet his eyes: pale green and fixed on me with intensity and expectation. His eyes and his blondness had surprised me when I'd first met him because I'd always thought Spanish people were dark.

'What is it?' he placed a hand on mine that felt firm yet easy. My knuckles were white with effort. I paused, took a breath. *Say it, say it now, just as you planned to.* But I didn't say it. I kissed him hard, so hard that our teeth banged together and my hands left the bed to clutch large fistfuls of his hair instead.

And for a time, nothing mattered outside of the room – Alex, our children but most of all, my resolve didn't matter – I was free to be weak, stupid, overcome ... the words to describe me go on and on.

But now it is afterwards, and yet again the outside world slowly encroaches, like a bloodstain. When I've told him, I will hurry home, do the garden and make sure that I phone the local Thai restaurant to order Alex's favourite takeaway for dinner tonight. Some might say I am trying to assuage my guilt, but I just want to be good, to be normal. I won't do anything like this again, I promise. I've got it all out of my system now, I'm sure of it.

My mobile beeps; rude and irritable, the suddenness makes my heart stutter. A text from Alex: Mal and Eleanor are coming for dinner at the weekend, so could I order some lamb from the organic farm shop? God, I hate Mal, so pompous and bigoted. Alex knows how I feel. So why does she do this?

As Javier stirs, I notice that the last mouthful of tea has a black powdery sludge at the bottom of the cup. I decide I can't face drinking any more then gulp it down anyway. I run my tongue over my teeth in case some of the residue had stuck to them and ponder that my wife has never questioned why sometimes I'm not in when she's called late or that I've started going out with friends I've never mentioned before.

Javier gets up from the bed and I watch him pull his clothes on over caramel coloured skin. I will miss his skin, his body, his mouth. *It's time.* We stand at the doorway together. I put a hand on his chest and I feel the hardness of muscles beneath his t-shirt; his wild hair brushes my cheek. As he pulls me to him, he murmurs Spanish in my ear. I can't quite catch it all, but I hear the last bit: '... next time, Daniel. My love.'

No, No, I scream inside.

'*Si, Si,*' I whisper back.

A SOLSTICE MOON

Suzie Sharpe

Laura Latimer loves Chester at Christmas. Wrapping her arms around a festively draped lamp post she steps off the kerb backwards, takes a swig from the bottle and wobbles diagonally across the uneven cobbles. The bells of the cathedral chime three.

Stopping in the middle of the deserted street she flexes her finger and winces. Blood is dried in the creases and it's swollen. Do fingers get gout? She sticks it in her mouth and gags as it touches her epiglottis. Or do they only puff up like this when you rip a wedding ring off and throw it at a selfish husband?

Her eyeballs bulge with a fresh threat of tears. France! He knew she hated garlic and mosquitoes. And Gauloises. And French toilets. And accordion players demanding money for playing at you when you didn't ask them to. Business trips she can tolerate. But living there?

She takes a moment negotiating the kerb on the opposite side of Northgate Street. When the streets are dark and silent Laura feels the centuries weave, crossing and changing. Breathing the magic of the city makes her heart beat faster.

'Each strand of the city's history,' she says aloud, narrowly missing a wooden bench, which she swears used to be somewhere else. 'Each strand,' she repeats, 'had twisted itself into the rope that bound her inexorably to the fabric of the city.' She heaves a sigh. 'She knew she could never leave.'

Staring up into the shadowed buttresses of St Werburgh's, she overbalances and clings to the railings for support. The cathedral crouches over her, making her scalp prickle. She shudders and grins up at it. At night the magenta sandstone is floodlit from beneath. Rather than accentuating the magnificence of the cathedral, the lighting sharpens the atmosphere of medieval menace that Laura has created in her *Black Abbot of St Werburgh* novels. Visiting fans still ask if it's fact or fiction. Laura generally smiles and says nothing. Anything is real if you want it to be.

She tiptoes past, so as not to wake the brotherhood.

'For a house of God,' she hisses in a stage whisper, 'you look like a bird of prey waiting to pick souls clean.' She raises an eyebrow and makes a mental note. That will be a great line for the current book. She runs her fingers along the railings, listening to the dying echo of her whispers. They crawl around the high walls, bouncing back at her, sounding like the blasphemous chanting of The Black Abbot himself.

The cobblestones of Eastgate Street each wear a circlet of frost. White Christmas lights criss-cross the precinct, reflecting a million twinkling diamonds in the icing sugar surfaces. It feels like stepping into an expensive Christmas card.

Laura's bottom lip trembles as she grabs the bottle from the pocket of her Barbour. There is an inch left, which she drains in one swig.

'Laura Latimer would die before leaving Chester,' she whispers, fresh tears burning her cheeks.

Outside the city walls, the road slopes gently towards the river. Laura crosses the main road and stares into the dark amphitheatre. Head on one side, she listens.

She marvels at the faint distant yelling of gladiators; the chanting to Nemesis, the roar of the crowd baying for blood. She feels as if she can't get enough air into her lungs. The veils begin to shift and merge; kaleidoscopic colours twist the neatly mown grass of the twentieth century; the stable wooden handrail and fence posts become ginger sand. The stone stepped arc of the arena pulses into being.

Turning slowly, she gasps at the first sight of the outline of St John's. The jagged fingers of the ruined eastern chancel strain upwards to touch a sliver of new moon. Her eyes fill with fresh tears.

A solstice moon.

She walks towards the church with the mechanical action of a sleepwalker. She feels the pull as it silently calls her, gently peeling back the layers of its past to reveal its roots, its ancient mysteries.

Slipping into the shadows behind the church she feels the familiar shift as time folds in on itself. The outline of the Lady Chapel blurs as the past vibrates with the present. Walls separate and thin, becoming a circle of tall oaks which melt away into an arcade of pillars.

Laura covers her ears with her hands. There are too many voices drowning the roar of crashing water as the River Dee rushes past, the swollen levels of ancient flood plains. She stumbles past the Lady Chapel, which shimmers and pulses as time twists its boundaries. Ploughing breathlessly into the ancient ruins of the chancel she flings herself across the altar and lies clinging to it. Closing her eyes, she waits.

The voices stop. The only sound is rushing water. She explores the smooth warmth of carved wood beneath her fingertips. Looking up, a sacred oak wound with mistletoe is standing at the centre of the grassy clearing. A young woman with a wild bush of russet hair threaded with ivy stands beside it, swathed in coarse white cloth. She is watching Laura.

'Neryedd,' Laura whispers. 'The veils are thin at the solstice.'

'Saturnalia is close. Why did you call me to you, Laura?'

'I've got to leave Deva. If I leave, I'll leave you. I'll never see you again.'

'I am spun from thy spirit.' Neryedd smiles. 'Where thy spirit travels, there shall you find me.'

'How?' Laura chokes back a sob, 'if I can't come to the Sacred Grove?'

'The Grove is from thy spirit also. You must seek its sanctuary within. The pathway less travelled …'

Laura remembers Neryedd using those words in *The Celtic Priestess*. She wondered what it meant when she wrote it twenty years ago. 'I don't understand,' she says, shaking her head.

Neryedd turns to walk away, fading until she is a shadow.

'Wait!' The grove turns around the altar. Laura screws her eyes tightly shut but it fails to blot out the whirling images, which strengthen and fade at frightening speed. The heroes and heroines of her novels fly in a wild dance of shifting shadows and voices, mixing and blurring times and places in a slamming explosion of noise.

It ends abruptly. Something loud is clanging in her ears and her heart is hammering painfully against her ribs. Feeling sick, she leans over the side of the altar and vomits whisky all over the English Heritage loose chippings. Sliding onto her backside, she stares up at the clock tower. Six o'clock. Her face is beaded with sweat and her brain is held in place by a carpenter's vice, clamped to her temples.

She wipes her forehead on the sleeve of her coat. Her finger hurts. And her teeth are clattering like a pneumatic drill, blurring her vision and sending shivering waves down the length of her body. She has slept. A layer of frost glitters on every surface. She pulls her collar around her neck, hugs her knees to her chest and closes her eyes.

Where thy spirit travels, there shall you find me, was what she said.

Does that mean you're not real, Neryedd? That I've imagined you?

You must seek its sanctuary within. The pathway less travelled.

Laura takes a deep breath, closes her eyes and visualises the Sacred Grove in sharp detail. The sound of gushing water; the sweet-smelling earth, smooth to the touch; the warmth of the raised ridges in the wood of the ancient altar, the great circle of oaks whispering above her ...

'Laura.' The clarity of the voice inside her head startles her.

But I'm only *thinking* you, Neryedd, she hears her imagined self saying. You're not real –

Only the present moment is true, Laura. All else is but memories.

You are a memory?

We are all but spirits of your creation.

I didn't imagine you, Neryedd. You showed me the ways of the ancients! We unravelled the mysteries of the past together –

The empowerment of your imaginings gives me substance, Laura.

Laura opens her eyes. 'What else have I made up?' she yells. 'My husband? My children? *Chester*?'

A youth staring at his phone, a dog on a lead at his side, is walking along the main road. He turns and stares at her for a moment before going back to his phone. A bus thunders by. Chester is awakening for the three shopping days before Christmas. Laura smiles as she walks across the crunchy grass towards home.

Her pace quickens as she walks past the cathedral. Maybe she should tell the family that Christmas is cancelled this year. We've got a lot to do if we're leaving for France in the New Year.

Anything can be real if you want it to be.

EVERYTHING IN THE WORLD

Elizabeth Brassington

I tucked the flower pot into my doll's pram. Today was its special treat.

Yesterday I was playing in the attic when I saw a book with Jesus on the front. I took it downstairs to Mummy and she read me a story from it. It was a story about a man who was hurt by robbers and nobody would help him. Then a man that nobody liked stopped and put bandages on him. The man was called the good samarington. Mummy said we should be like the good samarington and be kind to everyone.

When I went into the garden this morning, I was pushing my doll's pram when I thought of something really good. I would do what the good samarington did and be kind to everything in the world. I would give everything in the world a treat. I would tuck them all up in my doll's pram and give them a ride to the bottom of my garden and back. Everything in the world would have a turn.

I pushed the pram with the flower pot right to the end of the path, and when I came back again our two goats that are called Gert and Daisy were scrunching up grass on the lawn. They have nasty yellow eyes and I don't like them very much, but they had to have a treat like everything else. They were too big for the pram, so I threw them some bunches of juicy grass instead. I was wearing my sun suit that Mummy knitted for me with blue and yellow wool, and I was getting very hot. But I couldn't have a rest because I still had lots of treats to do.

The watering can had a turn next. It stuck out of the pram a bit and Gert gave me a funny look when I walked near to her. After that, I went into the kitchen because it was nice and cool there. Mummy was peeling potatoes and I told her what I was doing and how I'd done the flower pot and the watering can and the goats. She laughed and said that I had a long way to go yet, what was I going to do next?

I looked round the kitchen and saw the blue saucepan. It's my favourite because Mummy sometimes makes fudge in it when we've eaten our sweet rations. She once made me an Easter egg by squeezing some wet cocoa between two big spoons, so I thought I'd better choose the big spoons too. I took the saucepan and the spoons outside and put them in my pram. I hoped they wouldn't mind having to share the treat.

I did some more treats after dinner, and when it was bedtime I went straight to sleep because I was very, very tired.

In the middle of the night, I woke up because I heard the air raid warning go off. Granny calls it Wailing Willy. It always makes me think that someone is running after me, and I have to get out of the way before I get caught. It makes my tummy feel really funny. Mummy came up and put my dressing gown on and I picked up Ann, my best doll. She would break if you dropped her, so I didn't want a bomb to fall on top of her. We all went down to the shelter in the big cellar.

Granny won't go down to the cellar even if there is a very bad air raid. She says that they can come and get her if they want to. I hope they don't want to.

The shelter is made of very strong tin and is like a hut with a round-shaped roof. Daddy says it will keep us safe unless we have a direct hit. I hope we don't have a direct hit.

It's very dark on the cellar steps and Daddy has to carry me down, but there is a candle inside the shelter. It is kept in a tin so the light doesn't show. If you show a light, a bomb might hit you. Daddy has made a bunk bed for me which smells of sawdust and has a prickly army blanket on it.

I wanted to play Ludo instead of going to sleep, but I was so tired with all the treats I'd done that Daddy lifted me up onto my bunk bed and Mummy tucked me in. Just before I went to sleep, I heard a noise like lots of big lorries rumbling along in the sky. Daddy said, 'They aren't ours.' He calls them the Luftwaffer. Then the noise suddenly stopped and there was a big crashing sound. I heard Mummy whisper, 'That was a bit near,' and she sounded frightened, but then the all clear siren sounded and the next thing I knew, I was back in my bed and it was morning.

After dinner we had to go to the Co-op to fetch our rations, but when we got to the shops, the chemist's shop, which was near the Co-op, had been bombed out. It was Mr Prince's shop, but now there was just a big hole in the ground. It was filled with all sorts of broken things.

There was a soap shaped like a lemon that you would get for a birthday present, and lots of tins of Gibbs's Dentifriss. They are lovely shiny colours, red, blue and green, but now they were all squashed and ruined. Then I saw a bottle of Fennings Feever Cure, which Mummy gives me when I'm ill. It tastes really nasty, so I told Mummy I was glad that it was broken. She said that it was a pity, because it might have made a child that was really ill get better and that some nasty things could be really good in the end. I started to feel sorry for the bottle, but it was too broken to go in my doll's pram anyway.

We went to the Co-op for our rations, and when we got back home I took my pram out into the garden. I thought about the bottle of Fennings Feever Cure that was too broken to have a treat, and I decided that I would give something else that I didn't like a treat, to make up for it.

So I went upstairs to fetch my sailor doll, which I didn't like because his clothes were sewn on and I couldn't undress him. When I'd pushed him up and down the path, I put him in the sand pit so he could look at my sand pies. After that, I thought about what was going to have the next turn.

I thought really hard, and then I stood very still. I had just thought of something really nasty.

I couldn't give a treat to everything in the world.

If I gave a treat to everything in the world, one day I would have to give a treat to Hitler.

I left my pram and ran in to Mummy. 'Finished your good deeds?' she asked, smiling, and gave me a glass of milk and two biscuits.

PEBBLE'S VALEDICTION

Chris Hollis-Thompson

'Let's talk about ... death.'

The room is warm, but her hands feel cold. Enough for Tom to think about withdrawing his own. She rocks her head from side to side before she says the 'd' word like she's trying to come up with an alternative – something softer – but can't.

Instead of answering back, he nods. Unable to gauge how the conversation will go.

'You know Pebble's been sick for a long time,' she said. 'Or at least I'm assuming you noticed.'

He did. Pebble's been slower lately, less vibrant. Sleeps throughout the daytime. She would normally chase him around the house. Active and alert. Recently she seems more ... ashen.

Again, he nods.

'I did.'

'Right,' his mother says. 'That's because she's got a certain type of illness which doesn't ... well, it starts in one place then it spreads all over. You can't always fight it, however hard you try. They've tried everything to make her well, but I'm afraid it proved too difficult.'

His mother, though loving, never had much bedside manner. Can hide the truth, but can't sugar coat it. Tom nods for a third time without following her train of thought, wondering if and when he'll be allowed back into the other room. The television isn't paused, but he can wind his programme back.

'The fact is I haven't told you everything because you're too young to understand,' she says. 'Death is ...

well, it's a perfectly natural part of life so everything is fine. But it means Pebble had to go away.'

Her expression leads him somewhere he can't follow, which makes him feel uncomfortable. Tom takes his hands back after all.

'What are you saying?'

'Well ...' Her breath is drawn out. Her face pale. 'She's in the garage, Tom. You can say goodbye if you want, but I'm afraid she won't hear you. She wanted to –' His mum leans forwards and softens her tone. He can hear the parting of dry lips. 'She died this morning.'

She's right – Tom doesn't understand. He's only seven years old. But nevertheless, his legs go rigid like he forgot how to use them and a strange jolt runs down his backbone. He knows something significant has happened.

Focus shifts to the garage door. Plain, unassuming. Easy to disregard.

'In there?' he says.

'It was out here. But she's in there now.'

Tom doesn't consider how Pebble got from the kitchen to the garage. Maybe dead things always float out of the living space and into storage. He wouldn't know. The cartoons always cut away before stuff like that happens.

Just because his mother doesn't draw attention to it, the movement doesn't seem like a big deal. Instead, he stares at the door, and after some deliberation, she leans over to pull the latch. Slowly, with a creak, it drifts open. Sets the tone. Tom's fingers stiffen and point to the floor. There's a trailer in the garage, loaded with boxes. There's a bicycle and a trampoline, standing on its side. There's a pair of deckchairs. Some old paint tins.

In the middle of them all lies a red and white beach towel, flat across the bare concrete. Impossible to miss. And on top of that, to his shock and despair, is Pebble. A flat and lifeless lump, at once the same as ever yet completely different.

Tongue hanging out. Eyes open.

She looks horrible, instantly a shadow of her former self. And it's Tom's first taste of real death, which means he doesn't know how to react.

'Grandma?'

Pebble made it to eighty-nine, which Tom only learns at the funeral. He also learns her name was Patricia, nicknamed from the way he pronounced it as a baby. Everyone cries as the curtain falls on her wooden box, but he doesn't really understand why.

It means nothing.

In fact, he feels numb for a while. Life seems very different without her permanent fixture in the house. Tom's mother watches television with him for a few days before returning to work, but it's not the same. A child's home is a sacred place and sudden changes have a giant impact.

And he's only seven. At that age, death is something that happens to robots, monsters, the bad guys, the end of level boss, and his friend's baby sister when he shoots her with a plastic ray gun. It's an abstract, distant concept with no weight or consequence. A word people whisper, but never at bedtime.

Now all of that changes. Death has a face. Becomes tangible, and in the times he's left alone, it feels ever-present. Tom has too much time on his hands to pore over it. If Pebble can be reduced to a lump on a carpet with her tongue hanging out, then so can anyone. Family, friends, neighbours, schoolmates. His mother.

Himself.

He thinks about life's end for the first time. His impermanence becomes an inescapable, inevitable fact. Yet still a word no one speaks before bedtime. So does everyone know this already? He thinks back to when his Grandpa 'went away' years ago and realises what it actually meant.

Watching cartoons, he winces when the vampire chokes on daylight. Sees the horrible truth about zombies. When Hallowe'en comes around, it seems like a waking nightmare. He feels breathless in every moment, a tiny human on an incredibly huge ball of rock, floating in nothing much and for no reason. Hanging in the balance.

That's a lot to take in. A lot to digest. And for a time, Tom disappears inside himself to reconfigure his view of the world in general. To rewire his brain. To decide if he can accept what has probably been the truth all along.

'Pebble used to take her medicine.'

Tom is nine now, able to hear her name without going to a dark place. The opposite, in fact.

'Pebble used to spit it out when you weren't looking,' he says. 'Then she'd wink at me and smile.'

'Liar,' says his mother.

'Believe it.'

Time, it turns out, was all he needed. As the days roll by and the world keeps turning, Tom comes to accept death as a natural part of life. Just as his mother told him. It doesn't visit his house while he's sleeping to steal all of his loved ones away. It's not a daily occurrence.

It might not strike again for a very long time.

'You'll stay sick if you don't take what's on the spoon.'

'Then I'll tell her hello when I see her.'

'Only if you can stop coughing.'

His confidence healed with every cartoon he watched. Every robot, monster, bad guy, and end of level boss he saw perish. Every time he shot his friend's baby sister with a plastic ray gun.

Every time his mother made him laugh.

Now, he feels no sadness. They speak of Pebble often, and he's used to saying, 'she *was* this and that' rather than 'she *is* this and that.' A new normal is established, strange at first then less so. Sitting up in bed with a stinking cold, he uses memories of his Grandma for comfort.

'Pebble wouldn't need me to be able to speak. She could read my mind.'

His mother smiles. 'We all can, sweetheart. We all can.'

Given long enough, all negative feelings are forgotten. Blunted. But the positive ones remain, like diamonds emerging from the dirt. Tom no longer feels a weight upon his chest every time someone talks about their own grandparents. He's still got some, too. They just exist in the past instead of the present. Somewhere he can visit, but only in his mind.

And he thinks about his Grandma a lot. Takes the time to say hello. Pebble is sorry she can't be there. She still encourages him to be a boy and enjoy himself. Her voice makes comment on his cartoons. Doesn't always approve of the violence, just like when she was there in the living room. The memory of her is another part of him and he's better for it.

And though the last image of her may never leave him – eyes wide open, tongue hanging out – maybe that's okay.

Maybe death is a natural part of life.

Maybe he shouldn't worry about it.

Say hello to Grandpa, Pebble.

MERRYFIELDS SCHOOL 1996

Melanie Amri

I'm sent to Class 7 today. Stroking and Stretching's on the timetable.

Firstly, I'm assigned to John's tight tendons. I must straighten his arms. He's incontinent, epileptic, paraplegic and wheelchair-bound. He has 'severe and profound learning difficulties'. He's a tall, gaunt lad. Grey, vacant eyes.

A faint smell of stale urine and sweat pervades the air around us. A tape plays *Dancing in the Street,* softly in the background.

'We've been trying to straighten John's arms for years, can't we give him a break?' I ask Cheryl. I indicate John's pale and emaciated limbs; more bone than flesh. Both arms permanently bent at the elbow; stiffly upright and clamped to his chest: each clenched fist guarding a shoulder. 'I'm concerned that one day we'll accidentally cause a fracture.'

'Ugh-hh,' says John.

'No. We must have a positive attitude,' says Cheryl. 'Anyway we need something to write in his Record of Achievement.' Cheryl reaches down and strokes John's pallid skin. 'Cool,' she says. 'Now come on John, show Sandy how well you can work – you were a bit lazy yesterday, weren't you?'

'Ugh-hh!'

'Why don't we let our pupils have *fun*, for a change?' I persist.

Cheryl grimaces, making her look much older than her forty years. Her mousy hair hangs in thin tendrils around her face. 'We're not paid to let our pupils have fun, Sandy!'

I glance at the Star Chart on the wall – *For Those Who Have Worked Well Today*. Next to the names of the children, stuck-on gold stars glisten stoically in their paper galaxy.

I stroke John's arm.

'Cool,' says Cheryl as she clasps John's wrist and gently tries to pull it down, towards his knee.

'UGH-HH!' he frowns and resists.

'There, that's lovely!' Cheryl pats the recalcitrant elbow, 'good lad, John; you managed to straighten one of your arms for a bit longer today, didn't you? Sandy, can you write that please, in his Record of Achievement.'

I start to write.

'Now you'll get a certificate at the end of the year, John, and it'll be presented to you at our special Show and Shine Assembly!'

'Ugh-hh.'

I stroke and stretch and stroke and stretch. Cheryl watches me and says, 'Cool' and she gives me a vibrating massager. 'That might loosen him up even more,' then she goes to the other side of the classroom, to try to make Yasmin smile.

'Tell me if John's other arm gets a bit straighter,' she says, 'and I'll attempt to put a splint on it before it goes bent again.'

'Okay.' I place the massager on John's other arm. *ZZzzZZzz*. He grimaces. 'This is your special programme, John,' I whisper. *Zzzzzzz*. 'Sorry.'

'I heard that! Don't say sorry, Sandy. It's for his own good.'

'Oh, John's arm's getting straighter, Cheryl. Quick, before it stiffens up again!' Despite myself, I feel a sudden surge of joy.

'Cool! Good boy, John.' Cheryl claps her hands, vigorously. 'You see … it *does* work.'

But we still can't get the splint on.

Archie is three years old. He's got Down's syndrome. He has to sit strapped to a wooden chair. To straighten his back. He likes playing with the toys we put on the table in front of him. He loves thrashing around in the ball pool on Wednesdays.

Karen's crawling on the floor, next to Archie; she's dragging a naked – anatomically correct – boy doll along with her. Karen's a pretty child; she has curly blonde hair and limpid green eyes. She's wearing a pink tracksuit patterned with tiny red and white rosebuds. Her badge says *I am 5*. The words *Rose Garden Romance* are emblazoned across her little chest.

Karen wants to crawl around all the time. But she's not allowed. Her crawl is timetabled between 1.30pm and 2pm. Woe betide if she fancies a crawl before, or after.

Karen pulls herself up by Archie's chair, and snatches one of his toys. He reaches out and tugs her hair.

Karen screams, 'No!' And drops her doll.

Cheryl goes over to Archie and tugs at *his* hair. His face is blank. 'That's how it feels! WE HAVE KIND HANDS IN THIS CLASS. WE DO NOT HURT OUR FRIENDS IN CLASS 7!'

Archie stares at Cheryl and slaps her.

'Right!' She hauls him – still sitting in his chair – to a corner of the classroom, turns him round to face the wall, and removes his gold star from the Star Chart. 'You're spoilt,' Cheryl puts her face very close to his, 'thoroughly spoilt – and you think you can get away with the same behaviour at our school as you can get away with at home. Don't you?'

Archie stares at Cheryl and tries to slap her again. 'You naughty boy!' And she takes all his toys away.

Karen's crying and hugging her doll. Cheryl comforts her, puts her back in her chair and gives her the vibrating massager to play with. ZZZZzzzz. 'These kids'll be the death of me!' she says, 'I nearly lost it, just then – with Archie. You can only take so much, can't you?'

'Are things still difficult for you, Cheryl?'

'Yeah, no better. Paul's still shaggin' around and drinkin' as if there's no tomorrow. It's too much. I'd leave this job in a heartbeat, if I could.'

Karen drops the vibrating massager and screams.

ZZZZZZZZ the massager rotates on the floor, like a giant black bee, demented and vengeful. I pick it up and give it back to Karen and she instantly smiles. 'Yeah!' she says.

I put my hand on Cheryl's shoulder. 'It's not easy, is it?'

'You're not kiddin'! Oh well, there's not many places you can come to work and get free vibrators, is there?' She flushes and laughs.

I laugh too. But there's a flutter of anxiety in my chest.

'Anyway, what about you and Lassaad?' she asks me.

'Oh, you know, pink cloud of a marriage, as usual.'

'Yeah, right. Is he still gambling?'

I nod – and again that flutter of panicked wings in my rib cage, like a fettered bird.

'I want a wee, Cheryl.' Saleem screws his eyes up as if he's trying not to let any wee escape, from *anywhere*.

'You're not ready for a wee yet, Saleem, you've got to get into some kind of routine,' Cheryl snaps.

'Shall I do the names?' I ask her. 'I don't want to tread on anybody's toes … But it would give you a bit of a rest.'

Cheryl's face resembles a crushed paper bag.

'I need a wee – now!'

I notice a dark patch rapidly spreading over Saleem's crotch. 'Cheryl, Saleem's wet himself.'

'Oh for goodness' sake!'

'You can't expect the kids to have a routine for bodily functions, Cheryl.'

'Oh my f'ing God, if this class was left up to you, it would be chaos. It's all right for you part-timers!'

'Okay, do you want me to change Saleem, or shall I try to make Yasmin smile?'

'Cool. Just tick the box will you, on Yasmin's Record of Achievement – to say she smiled – and then will you do the names? I'll change Saleem. I bloody would like to change him, I can tell you!' says Cheryl, sotto voce. Then she hauls Saleem out of his chair. 'You sit there all day, don't you, Saleem? Like King Tut, expecting Sandy and I to wait on you – hand and foot.'

'Yes, Cheryl. Sorry Cheryl,' Saleem whimpers. And he shuffles to the Changing Area, clinging to Cheryl's arm as if it were a life jacket.

I tick Yasmin's SMILE box in her Record of Achievement, even though we've not seen her smile since 1990. Then I gather the children into a semicircle. I hold up a card with each child's name on. Every card has a piece of fabric stuck to it.

'Is Karen here?' I say, in the loud, exaggerated falsetto voice that we use at Merryfields.

'No!' says Karen.

'Yes, you *are* here Karen.' And I help her stroke the black velvet fabric next to her name. Then it's John's turn. I place the nylon on his cheek and gently guide his hand. Archie's fabric is wool. He tries to eat it. Saleem is still in the Changing Area. So we all take a turn at stroking his fabric for him. I can't find Yasmin's card.

'Where's Eliza, everyone?'

'Ugh!' says John.

'Here!' shouts Karen.

'No, Eliza's not here. She's very poorly … She's in hospital. So shall we sing a song for Eliza?'

'Want dwink.'

'Yes, Karen, we'll all have a nice drink and some fruit, after the song.'

'Want dwink!' She starts to cry.

I grab a tambourine and sing this week's hymn, '*This Little Light of Mine, I'm Gonna let it Shine! This Little Light of Mine, I'm Gonna let it Shine! Let it Shine, Let it Shine, Let it Shine!*' Yasmin opens her mouth in a sort of grin, and rocks to and fro in her wheelchair. Her azure blue sari flows around her like a small, tropical sea.

And the sunlight pushes itself through the blind-slats at our classroom window, bathing us all in a soft, reverential glow.

AN ENDING

Melanie Cheung

For a brief moment, as the sunlight passes behind him, I get a glimpse of the boy I used to know. He's there in the slope of the shoulders, in the indifferent sweep of his hair. Then, all too soon, the recollection dissolves, and it's only some stranger sat on the bed opposite me, fumbling with his shirt buttons.

I take a final drag from my cigarette before stubbing it out in the trinket dish, my fingernails collecting ash. From my seat on the floor I am well placed to study him. He squints as he reaches the final button under his chin, and as his head bows forward there is excess flesh there that I don't remember. His whole body seems to have swelled, as though someone took a finger and smudged his edges. I see where he's beginning to grey as the last of the light catches the side of his head. His hands seem clumsy. Perhaps he is nervous? No. He is feeling guilty. I can see it as he flips his tie over itself, and then with an impatient tug he fixes the noose.

'I can make you something to drink. Tea, coffee? Before you go.'

He shakes his head gently, and in what feels like an apology, offers a vague smile to the space between us. He has not looked at me since I drew the curtains back, and where a moment before I might have put this down to shyness, now I'm not so sure. I crawl over to him on my hands and knees. I'm not trying to be seductive. There is in that narrow distance between us an unspoken civility that I feel would fracture under excessive movements. Standing or walking would be careless of me.

'When do you have to go?' I ask, crossing my arms on his lap. He raises his watch level with my head, his eyes avoiding mine.

'Soon. I can't miss the train.'

I nod and reclaim my arms.

'Okay, but I'll make coffee anyway.' I get up and don't look back to check if he is in agreement.

In the kitchen I switch the kettle on and settle into this reprieve. Now we both have the safety of an entire room to ourselves. His jacket hangs squarely on the back of a chair. Without a thought I walk over to it and grab at the pockets to guess at their contents. I feel the bulk of his wallet and take it out. Flipping it open I see two toddler-aged boys smiling back at me. I cover their faces with my thumb and slide out credit cards, receipts, and membership cards. I don't feel anything as I scan over the numbers and letters formed in neat lines and arranged in lists. It's as though I am looking at the bottom of a cluttered drawer. Whatever clues they might offer to that life sitting on my bed in the next room are obscured from me, so I quietly return the wallet to its pocket.

The kettle switch flips up. As I stir in the milk I realise that I'm only wearing my underwear. I look around for something to hide myself in; I don't want to appear flippant. I tiptoe across to the bathroom door and reach around for the robe that I know is hanging on the other side. Before I can find my way through the sleeves he steps into the room. I dart into the bathroom and call out, 'The coffee is next to the sink.' As I tie the cord slowly around my waist I listen to his footsteps as he steps across the room.

'I don't drink coffee much, it would be a shame to waste it.' Panic has entered my voice. I'm scared he has heard it too, but when I leave the bathroom he is leaning casually against the counter, the cup in his hand.

I attempt to commit this image to memory. A keepsake for me. But I'm trying too hard and I can barely remember him as he stands across from me.

'This is a nice area, right in the middle of the city. Do you like living here?'

'It's okay,' I shrug. I want to say more, to show that I can be casual about this whole thing too, but my mind falls blank.

He looks at me, or rather stares through me, searching, as I did in the bedroom, for something that is familiar, makes sense, to him. I straighten up, presenting myself fully to his wordless interrogation.

'I can't come back.'

'I understand,' I say, the panic in my voice returning.

'It's just,' he looks up to the ceiling light, as though the right response might fall down on him, 'I never meant for this to happen, I'm not sure how it has.'

'I understand. It was a mistake. Tomorrow it won't mean anything.' The words slip out so easily that I know I'm lying. He swills back the coffee, his face wincing from the heat. It's a small gesture; I'll drink your coffee and let there be no hard feelings. I should return it by walking over to the door, to show that I accept his leaving my life for the second time, but I don't move from where I'm standing in front of the bathroom. While he puts on his jacket I weave the cord of my robe through my fingers, one time, two times.

'I'm leaving now,' he whispers. 'I'm not coming back. Do you understand?'

I nod at my bare feet. The blur of his hand reaches out for me but then he thinks better of it and withdraws. I wait to hear the door close but when I finally look up he has gone and the door is ajar. I dart over to the window and count the seconds I think it will take him to get down three flights of stairs and out of the front door. He appears on the street before I've finished counting and doesn't look back as he is absorbed into the early evening crowds. I watch him walking away with that peculiar stride, like a cork bobbing up and down on the water.

And there he is again, the boy I used to know.